CLEAN SWEEP

Squeaky Clean Mysteries, Book 14

CHRISTY BARRITT

"So you'll never believe what I discovered." I turned toward my best friend, Sierra, as we sat on the bleachers of an oversized gymnasium that smelled of sweat, chlorine, and hundreds of dreams writhing in agony on their deathbeds.

Sierra and I had met here to watch my husband, Riley, compete at a ninja warrior-style competition. It was an obstacle course that tested competitors' strength, agility, balance, and stamina through a series of challenges—from rock walls to extreme monkey bars, balance beams, and more.

Riley had done great in the preliminaries and would be moving on to the next round of competition in a couple weeks. Unfortunately, 90 percent of the competitors hadn't. Some of them now punched walls, one cried, and another stared in mourning at the obstacle course while his friends patted his back.

It was quite the sight.

Sierra ran a hand through her sleek, black hair. Her Asian genes had created the perfect texture and sheen. I was just a little jealous, especially since my genes had created the hair texture and sheen of someone who'd stuck their finger in a light socket.

"You're keeping me in suspense here, Gabby. What did you discover?"

I turned away from the competition and glanced at her. "I just found the perfect product to help smooth my frizzy hair."

"Okay . . . what's this product?" Sierra shifted ten-month-old Reef, her son, to her other leg, but her gaze volleyed back and forth from Reef, to the crowds, to me.

I could tell I didn't have her full attention. Perhaps I hadn't had her full attention since she'd become a mom. I figured that was par for the course after someone entered the new and exciting world of parenthood.

"It's argan oil," I continued. I'd been dying to tell her this story. In fact, I'd mentally rehearsed the best, most compelling way to share this information a million times, each one more satisfying than the last. "Maybe you've heard of it? Anyway, it turns out the oil is produced from these kernels that fall from an argan tree."

The announcer in the background was ruining the overall

atmosphere for the story. He was so loud I could hardly hear myself. And then there was the cheering around us as people rooted for their favorite competitors. This was a whole different world for me. A world of athleticism. Competition. And adults who reminded me of kids challenging each other on the playground . . . only for a ten thousand-dollar prize.

I kept my eyes open for Riley, who'd already finished the obstacle course. Since he'd come through with flying colors, I was anxious to tell him what a good job he'd done. Last time, I'd blown it by giving him a nickname— the Leaping Lizard. Apparently, that wasn't flattering. Who would have thought? I'd thrown away the shirt I'd gotten made before he saw it. No, from here on out, he'd have a masculine name like the Gorging Gorilla or Lithium Lion.

Or not.

I was still working on it. Every competitor had a catchy nickname, and I didn't want my Riley to feel left out.

"I keep thinking this conversation is going somewhere, but my certainty is growing uncertain." Sierra frowned and bounced Reef on her knees.

I snapped my attention back to my friend, feeling like I had a bit of ADHD right now. "Sorry. Anyway, like I said, it turns out that these argan kernels are hard to process. So guess what these people do? They let goats eat the argan kernels, and then they dig the kernels out of . . .

wait for it. Wait for it. They dig the kernels out of the . . . excrement."

Sierra let out a loud laugh, her gaze fully on me for a good five seconds. That was a record lately. "You've got to be kidding?"

"No, there's something about me liking things made from poop lately. I don't get it." Not long ago, a friend had introduced me to kopi luwak, and it turned out the delicious coffee was made from cat turds.

I just couldn't win lately. Maybe someone was trying to teach me a deep life lesson. Something like: when life hands you poop, make coffee or haircare products.

"You're so funny, Gabby." Sierra pushed her glasses up higher on her tiny nose.

I leaned closer to Reef, who was trying to eat his mom's thus-said sleek, shiny, perfect hair. The boy's wide eyes soaked everything in with an innocence that melted my heart. "And you're so cute, Little Man."

He babbled in response.

Just then, Riley appeared from the locker-room area. I stood, ready to give him a congratulatory kiss. But before I even took a step, my gaze fell on a man walking beside him. I recognized Riley's new friend from the competition. He'd gone two people ahead of Riley and had done well, also making it through to the next round.

I excused myself from Sierra for a moment, managed to make it down the metal bleachers without falling on my face—that was always a plus—and wound my way through the crowds toward my handsome husband.

Husband.

Every time I said the word—whether mentally or out loud or in my dreams—it made me smile. I couldn't believe I'd actually gotten the guy. *The* guy. The one I'd pined over, dreamed about, and nearly given up hope on. Sometimes, life did work out the way you wanted.

Riley spotted me, waved, and we met amidst a sea of cheering inner-city kids supporting their basketball coach on the course. I gave Riley a quick kiss on the cheek, noting the fresh scent of Ivory soap. He must have just showered. His clean blue T-shirt and black athletic shorts should have been the first sign.

"Good job out there, Whistling Weasel."

Riley gave me a look.

"Flying Squirrel?"

He continued to stare.

"Soaring Eagle?"

"Just Riley is great." He looked subtly amused—at least that's what I told myself—before stepping back. "Gabby, I'd like to introduce you to my friend, Conrad Murphy."

I quickly soaked in the man beside Riley. Conrad was on the shorter side—probably around my height of five feet five inches. He had blond hair cut in one of those trendy styles with short sides, a hard part, and a gelled poof at the top. Muscular and pensive were the first two words that came to mind when I saw him.

The good news was that I hadn't mentally described him as an animal, which was what I usually did. Apparently, people didn't find that very flattering. So no way would I tell anyone that this guy reminded me of a chipmunk who'd just been to the beauty salon. Oops . . . there I went again.

Introductions went around.

And when the round finished, I was left with the definite feeling that both Riley and Conrad were waiting to say something of significance. The awkward moment of silence gave it away. People didn't say I was good at investigating for nothing.

"Do you have time to do lunch with us?" Riley held onto the towel around his neck as he waited for my answer. "Conrad has a story that I think you'll be very interested in hearing."

I needed to finish unpacking at our new place, and, apparently, I needed to figure out paint colors. But I knew nothing about decorating or complementing color schemes that might make our place look fit for a lawyer with persnickety, unapproving parents. So putting off those tasks and having lunch instead? It sounded great.

Riley and I had just bought our first house. It wasn't anything fancy, but it did have character and charm, and I already loved it. We'd closed on the place three weeks ago, but we were still unpacking. Riley and I had been so busy with our jobs that house stuff had taken a back burner.

"Of course I can do lunch." I stole another glance at Pensive Conrad, wondering just what was behind this conversation. Since I was inherently nosy, I couldn't wait to find out.

"I'm going to take off." Sierra grabbed her keys from an oversized diaper bag with bears and zebras all over it, along with a small "Save the Animals" emblem in the corner. "It's almost Reef's naptime anyway. Good seeing you all—and nice meeting you, Conrad."

As much as I hated to see her go, I couldn't wait to find out what all this was about.

I didn't have Spidey senses. No, I had Sherlock senses.

And they didn't tingle.

No, they fired at full force like a genius with OCD who didn't let one detail slip past.

I peppered Riley on the drive to the restaurant about what Conrad's story was. But he wouldn't tell me. He wanted me to hear it from Conrad himself. So I tried to wait patiently—something I wasn't very good at doing.

We picked a restaurant just down the street, a café that was known for its biscuits, of all things. After we ordered and got our drinks and made the usual rounds of chitchat about crime in the area—wait, that was normal, right?—I was ready to get down to business.

But I didn't want to be rude. Of course. So I sat quietly and waited for Riley and Conrad to get the hint.

"Riley tells me you're quite the investigator," Conrad started. He'd foregone getting water or a soda and had brought his own energy drink instead. He'd also wiped down the entire table with his napkin, perfectly lined up his silverware, and organized the salt, pepper, hot sauce, and sugar packets.

"I have a few cases under my belt."

"She's being humble." Riley draped his arm casually across the back of my chair. "Gabby's sought after when it comes to anything investigative. She works for the leading US forensic company and teaches other law enforcement personnel how to do their jobs."

"That might be overstating it a bit."

"She's also solved more crimes than most of the professionals I've met," Riley continued.

"That might be true." I tried to sound humble but confident, which was a more difficult balance than it might seem.

"It's like God made her to be nosy and ordained that nosiness to be incredibly helpful," Riley finished.

"Well, aren't those just the sweetest words you ever said?" I batted my eyelashes before grinning at Conrad. "And this is why I fell in love with him."

The glimmer of amusement in the man's eyes was

fleeting. He drew in a deep breath and leaned back in his chair. "I was telling Riley a bit of my story earlier."

The man didn't seem to notice anything else around him. Not the hustle and bustle of a group of college kids who'd come in or the baby crying two tables over or the waitress who kept stealing looks at his chiseled chipmunk physique. No, mentally Conrad was somewhere far from this place.

"My wife, Brooke, disappeared four months ago, and the police have pretty much given up on finding her." Conrad's voice cracked.

My heart lurched into my throat at his stark words and the absolute despair in his voice. "That's horrible. I'm so sorry."

He nodded, but the action looked heavy and almost painful. "I haven't given up hope that she'll turn up."

I laced my hands together. Conrad had my entire attention now. "Tell me more. Tell me about her disappearance."

He let out a breath and pushed his drink away.

Before he could start, the flirting waitress delivered our food. I'd ordered chicken salad with pecans and a berry compote over a dense, buttery biscuit. The dish itself was a masterpiece and looked—and smelled—absolutely delicious. I was far more interested in Conrad's story, though.

"Brooke is a nurse." Conrad picked at the top of his biscuit. "A great nurse. She worked in labor and delivery, and she loved her job. On the day she disappeared, she left for work in the morning, just like any other day. Nothing seemed strange or out of the ordinary."

"What do you do for a living, Conrad?" I was trying to get the big picture of their life together before delving into the details of what happened.

Those details might not seem important, but they were. They wove a tapestry of a person's life, and you never knew which thread would be the one that held the whole thing together or pulled it all apart.

"I'm a teacher."

It wasn't what I would have guessed, not based on his trendy style or uptight demeanor. But okay. "Do you have any kids?"

"No, but Brooke and I had been trying for the past few years. We were about to do some fertility testing and maybe consider IVF."

That meant a lot of money and probably a lot of stress as well. I also couldn't help but think how hard that might be for Brooke—to work in labor and delivery, to want a child, but not to be able to conceive. It would be like a food addict working in a candy store or an alcoholic being a bartender.

"Okay, continue." I took a bite of my biscuit, and the buttery taste mingled with the crunch of the pecans and the sweetness of the berry compote. It was heavenly.

"Anyway, Brooke left work that day at her normal time. The police confirmed that. She told one of her coworkers that she was going to run a couple of errands before heading home. And that was the last anyone saw of her."

I blinked at the abruptness of it, of how life could go from normal to devastating faster than a snake striking its prey. The case also sounded vaguely familiar, as if I'd heard parts of it on the news.

"Did police check the camera footage in the parking lot at the hospital?" I asked.

"Yes, and there was no sign of foul play. Brooke got into her car and left without any issues."

So where had the woman gone? And had she disappeared on purpose or had someone persuaded her to head somewhere else? Hopefully, the persuasion wasn't of the violent nature because I really preferred cases that ended with happiness instead of sorrow. Avril Lavigne seemed to agree. She sang "Happy Ending" on the overhead speakers. Which was actually a song about not getting a happy ending, but I'd overlook that.

"Did she have one of those transponders in her car for tolls?" Riley asked. "Sometimes police can use those to track people's vehicles."

Conrad shook his head. "No, we didn't have one, and we didn't have any of those built-in GPS systems either. Her car was found a week later in a parking garage at the oceanfront in Virginia Beach—one that tourists going to the beach usually use. There were no cameras in that area that proved to be helpful."

Interesting. "So maybe someone knew that and picked that location on purpose."

Or Brooke knew that. I wasn't jumping to any conclusions. Not yet.

Conrad moved from picking at his biscuit to rubbing the side of his plate. This was hard for him. Really hard.

"Were the police able to trace her cell phone?" I asked, trying to keep him talking before grief consumed him.

"It was found in a ditch off the interstate. Her records showed two calls from an unknown number. One was from the Thursday before she disappeared, and the next was from the Monday she was last seen. Unfortunately, the calls were from a burner phone so the police couldn't trace it."

"And you didn't recognize the number?" Riley popped a cucumber with hummus into his mouth.

The man was always starving after competing, but Riley was obviously wrapped up in this story too because he hadn't touched his food until just then. The amount of calories Riley burned at these competitions was comparable to trash being incinerated at a waste disposal plant. I was a little jealous.

"I didn't recognize the number from the burner phone," Conrad said.

I took another bite of my biscuit, using my fork just to be polite. "Do the police have any leads or theories on what happened?"

Conrad's face darkened like a pop-up thundershower

on an already cloudy and miserable day. "No . . . well, yes. They suspected . . . me."

My throat tightened, even though his statement wasn't unexpected. "Why was that?"

He rubbed his forehead before his arm came down harder than necessary on the table. "Brooke and I had been arguing lately. Infertility was taking a toll on us. We both worked—probably too much—under the guise of trying to get ahead and prepare for having a baby, whenever that happened. In truth, maybe we were trying to avoid reality. But I would never hurt Brooke, despite our faults as a couple and my own faults as a man."

"I see." I appreciated his honesty, and I hoped that was what he was giving me—the truth. I'd been lied to a lot, though, and nothing really surprised me anymore.

Conrad shifted in his seat, as if about to share something uncomfortable. "The other thing is this: I keep feeling like I'm being watched."

I tilted my head. "What do you mean?"

"I mean . . . it's nothing I can prove. But ever since Brooke disappeared, I've felt like someone has eyes on me."

"And you think this has something to do with your wife's disappearance?" I clarified.

Conrad shrugged. "I don't know. I have no idea, actually. I just wanted to mention it in case it was relevant."

It certainly added another interesting dimension. "I suppose it could be connected."

"Look, it's like this. The police ran out of leads. Out of evidence. And now I just feel like they've given up. Brooke's parents hired a PI, but he gave up also. When Riley told me about you, I thought . . ." Conrad shrugged and released a long, drawn-out sigh. "I thought maybe you could help. I'm desperate, really."

I didn't have to think very hard about how to proceed because I loved investigating, and I loved helping people. "I'd be more than happy to help you, Conrad."

Some of the tension seemed to leave his shoulders, and they drooped. "I don't know how much you charge. I don't have much money, though. I know I sound like a mess." He ran a hand over his face. "And I was a mess. The past few months have been dark, to say the least. These competitions have helped me turn my life around."

My brain gears were already going. "I'm not very concerned about money. In fact, I think I may have a solution for that. I just need to make a few phone calls."

CHAPTER TWO

I sat in my dining room, at a little card table that Riley and I were temporarily using, and stared at the papers in front of me. I'd been scribbling notes for the past thirty minutes.

Deciding to take a break, I leaned back and glanced around me.

I still couldn't believe this house was mine.

Mine.

Well, mine and Riley's. The craftsman-style abode was a humble beauty with white siding, a picket fence, and a wide porch with a swing. Inside were nooks, crannies, built-in bookcases, and gorgeous wood floors. Outside was a large backyard with a small guesthouse, and where the grass ended, the Lafayette River began.

I was still staring at the house when Riley stepped from the hallway, ready to go . . . somewhere.

I sucked in a deep breath. Our Saturday evening date. How had I forgotten? Our goal was to make this a priority every week.

I still wore my old jeans and my favorite "Never Trust an Atom: They Make Up Everything" T-shirt. I hadn't looked in the mirror lately, but I'd bet my hair was a wild mess of curls. And I'd donned flip-flops, which might not be so bad except my toenail polish was chipped and ragged looking.

Gabby for the win . . .

Riley pulled a chair close, sat beside me, and folded his lean, muscular arms over each other on the card table. He'd always been handsome, but ever since he'd suffered a gunshot wound to the head, he'd changed. During recovery, he'd taken a new focus on his health, and now all his features seemed more defined and sculpted.

"You look a little dressier than I do," I said with an apologetic frown.

"We were going to try that new restaurant downtown."

"Yes, we were. I mean, we are," I quickly corrected. "I just need to change real fast."

"You're thinking about Conrad, aren't you?" Riley studied my face.

I frowned again, guilty as charged. "You know me."

"Yes, I do. What did you find out?"

I looked at the doodles and random notes that probably no one else but me could decipher. "Well, as you know, Conrad stopped by earlier with the case file. We have it only because Brooke's parents hired a PI, and he was able to get his hands on the official documents. They made copies of the files for Conrad."

"That's helpful."

"It is. He also gave me the names of some of Brooke's friends and family members. I still don't really have enough information to go on. But I did call Garrett, and he gave me the go-ahead for this case."

Garrett Mercer was a multi-millionaire who funded the cold-case squad, as I called it. He'd put the money into the project after his own family had been murdered. I'd helped solve the case ten years after it happened, and Garrett had been one of my biggest fans since then.

This case wasn't officially cold, but all the leads had dried up. It was unsolved, and that was close enough for Garrett. That meant it was close enough for me too.

"That's good news," Riley said.

"I also called Evie and Sherman. They're going to see how quickly they can get here." Evie Manson and Sherman McDonald were two of my colleagues who helped with the cold-case squad. Evie was a brilliant forensic psychosociologist, and Sherman knew the inner workings of a computer like Christiann Huygens knew a clock. Um . . . he was the guy who invented clocks, FYI.

I'd last seen Evie and Sherman in January when they came to Virginia for a case over on the Eastern Shore. It was the beginning of March now, so a good six weeks had passed since we'd last seen each other.

"Also good news," Riley said.

"And . . . I was able to talk to the detective on the case. He's going to meet with me tomorrow after church." I tried to space out my progress so I wouldn't overwhelm Riley. I had a tendency to do that sometimes. "He won't be able to share much other than what's on the news and public knowledge."

"You've been one busy girl."

"Yes, I have been." I sighed. "Missing persons cases fascinate me."

"Every case fascinates you."

"I can't argue with that." I couldn't resist leaning closer and pressing my lips into his. Riley caught me at the waist and tugged me closer, not in any hurry to move away.

Until someone pounded on the door. I'd recognize that knock anywhere. Based on Riley's look, so did he.

I followed behind Riley as he rose to answer. When he pulled the door open, I saw Bill McCormick standing on our porch with a wide grin on his pudgy face. He looked rumpled, as if he'd just gotten off a plane. Then again, he always looked rumpled.

But his voice was as smooth as honey, and that was most important in his line of work.

"I'm back from the book tour!" he announced with a wide flourish of his hands that indicated a future in

Broadway might be an option if his current career didn't work out. "It was a raging success."

"That's great, Bill," I said.

His radio talk show had soared in popularity in recent months, propelling him to a new level of fame. He'd also just bought the oversized house next door to Riley and me.

Which I had mixed feelings on.

I mean, I liked Bill. But he could be overbearing. And his house was so out of place in this neighborhood full of cozy bungalows. I'd heard the dwelling originally at that site had been condemned and torn down. Someone had bought the land and built a three-story brick veneer home to replace it. Every time I looked at it, I couldn't help but think about those cartoon drawings in children's magazines where one had to find everything that was out of place in the scene. Even a toddler could pick out Bill's place.

Since Chad and Sierra were temporarily living in our tiny guesthouse, and Bill was living next door, it almost felt like the gang from our old apartment building was back together and the old times had merged into a new and improved current times.

The only person missing was Mrs. Mystery, who'd been our upstairs neighbor. She'd decided to move down to Florida for the winter. She thought the change of scenery might offer inspiration for her next book.

From the corner of my eye, I saw Chad, Sierra, and

Reef moseying from around the side of the house, a pizza box in Chad's hands. No doubt, it had a vegan specialty inside. I'd actually discovered some of those cruelty-free recipes weren't all that bad.

"We're here for the party," Chad said.

"What party?" I asked, trying to figure out what I'd missed.

Sierra switched Reef to her other hip. "Bill told us you were having a party."

My gaze went to Bill, and he shrugged. "Sorry, I should have told you first that it's at your place. But we have a lot to celebrate."

"Do we?" Riley slid his hand around my waist and pulled me closer.

I knew what he was doing. He was trying to protect our date night. And to stop me from saying something I shouldn't.

"Well, we all have new places to live," Bill started.

"Our house is actually being built," Sierra corrected. "My arrangement is temporary."

"Tom*a*to, toma*to*." Bill waved her off. "We all have new beginnings."

"Really just new places to live," Riley said. "Everything else is the same."

"And . . . my book just hit the *New York Times* bestseller list!"

Congratulations went around.

For the next two hours, our date night turned into a

party with some of our strangest, dearest friends. As we all ate and talked and shared life together, I paused and stood back for a moment.

My mind went back to Brooke, and I tried to put myself in her shoes. What would my life have to look like in order for me to walk away from it? A fight with Riley? A future that felt or looked hopeless? Feeling like I was around people yet alone?

I didn't know what Brooke was thinking—or even if she had walked away.

I only knew I couldn't think of one reason I'd want to abandon this life right now. And I hoped I never could.

The next day after church, Riley and I parted ways. We normally tried to spend the day together, but right now I needed to get a jump-start on this investigation, and he needed to train for the final leg of the competition. I was going to try and get as much done today as possible.

I started by meeting with Detective Chris Belfield at a police precinct in Virginia Beach.

I'd worked hard to develop a good relationship with the local police, especially since early in my job as a crime-scene cleaner I'd blown it several times. I'd pushed my way into investigations where I wasn't welcome. I'd inserted my opinions when no one wanted to hear them.

I'd maybe even trespassed at a crime scene on more than one occasion.

I wasn't above doing that again, but since I'd matured —insert dramatic throat clearing—I'd decided to try and take the high road.

I didn't know this detective well, but he seemed competent enough when we spoke on the phone yesterday. Meeting him now, I noted he was tall with dark skin and a piercing gaze. He was probably in his early thirties, and he wore a wedding ring.

I'd seen him pull a pacifier out of his pocket as we'd walked down the hallway, looking perplexed as to how it had gotten there. I assumed he was a sleep-deprived parent of an infant. I recognized it because of Sierra and Chad. Complete and utter exhaustion was their new look.

After getting coffee together from the break room, Belfield sat at the end of a long, glossy table in the precinct's conference room. I sat one chair away—a respectable distance.

"What can I do to help you?" he started. "I'd love more than anything to close this case, and I know you have the credentials to offer a new perspective on this investigation."

"Thank you," I said, feeling nearly giddy at his accolades but trying not to show it. "I've read the case file— Mr. Murphy gave me a copy of it. A PI was able to obtain the files. I'd love to hear what happened from your point of view. Who were your persons of interest—

officially or unofficially? What motives did you suspect?"

He let out a small breath before making eye contact with me. "The disappearance of Brooke Murphy was a strange case from the start. Like most investigations of this sort, we suspected the husband."

"Why did you suspect him?"

"There had been some tension between him and his wife. Neighbors said they heard the couple arguing quite heatedly on more than one occasion."

That added a new perspective to this. Then again, Conrad had said their marriage wasn't perfect.

"Sounds like a potential motive to me," I said. "Did Conrad—Mr. Murphy—take out an insurance policy?"

It was so cliché, yet it happened. I'd seen it before.

"When the couple started trying to conceive three years ago, an insurance policy was taken out. But Mr. Murphy said that was because he and his wife hoped to change their family's status from two to three. It's not entirely unusual."

"Makes sense."

"And then there was the fact that Mr. Murphy appears to have an alibi," Detective Belfield continued. "He was in a photography class at the time his wife disappeared. Several people saw him there. Said they saw him trying to call his wife and heard him remark that he was becoming concerned she wasn't answering."

Photography? Okay. That was unexpected.

"Is there a chance he could have slipped away from this class?" I asked. "Criminals have been known to do it before."

Detective Belfield let out a long breath. "We don't believe so, although he was there for two hours. Part of the time—about thirty minutes—he was supposedly in the woods doing some landscape photos. Was that long enough to do something? Maybe. But I doubt it."

I took a sip of the police department coffee and tried not to cringe. Man, that stuff was bad. Really bad. "Were there any other suspects?"

"We looked into an ex-boyfriend who'd remained friends with Mrs. Murphy. We explored the possibility that she stumbled into some gang activity taking place in the area where her vehicle was found. We also explored the possibility that Mrs. Murphy just left. That she wanted to disappear and start a new life, so she walked away."

That sounded pretty thorough. "Did any of those pan out?"

"Unfortunately, no. Every lead dried up. The ex-boyfriend had an alibi. The gang wouldn't have hidden their deed—they'd flaunt it. As far as Mrs. Murphy disappearing on purpose, I suppose that could still be a possibility. We haven't had any hits on her credit card, and, as far as we know, she hasn't been in touch with any of her family members."

It was entirely possible for someone to disappear. The question was: Was it by her own doing or someone else's?

Famous cases flashed into my memory, beginning with one in Maine. A woman went to visit her sister but never showed up. Authorities were called in. It turned out her husband thought she was having an affair, killed her, and buried her body in a field five miles from their home.

Then there was the Arizona mom who was abducted by strangers while she was jogging. She managed to escape a month later. It turned out her abductors were part of a cult.

The truth was, in this digital age, it seemed like everyone left some kind of trail, so completely disappearing on your own was a huge undertaking. No online or financial hits in four months? Unless Brooke was a master of covering her tracks, that seemed suspicious in itself.

"Is there anything else that might be relevant to this investigation?" I glanced at my coffee and briefly considered taking another sip before deciding it wasn't worth it. "That you're authorized to share, of course."

Detective Belfield shifted in his seat, a light flickering in his eyes—almost as if this was the one question that excited him. "We did discover that Brooke had racked up quite a bit of debt."

And now introducing money and love—two of the main motives behind crimes. "How much debt are we talking?"

"Almost twenty thousand dollars."

My eyes widened. That was a decent chunk of change. "On what?"

"Clothes. Jewelry. Spa days. Mrs. Murphy grew up with quite a bit of money. And her husband was a teacher, so they weren't exactly wealthy. The surprising thing was that her husband didn't appear to know about the debt until a week before she disappeared."

"Is that right?" And a week later she was gone? That didn't look good.

Although, I had to say, Conrad's grief *had* appeared real and true.

I was going to have to ask him about those details. And I hoped he'd be straight with me.

CHAPTER THREE

I called Conrad after I left the police station, and he agreed to meet with me that evening at the gym where he and Riley worked out. I could have just talked to him on the phone, but I wanted to see his face. Waiting would be worth it.

In the meantime, I'd called Brooke's friends from the list Conrad had given me. Most of them sounded sad but had no information to offer me. I moved on from calling them to looking up Brooke's social media accounts. I messaged a couple of her friends there, including a woman named Macy Williamson.

Macy seemed eager to chat, like the take-a-bull-by-the-horns kind of woman. She was available for a late lunch/early dinner, which sounded good to me.

Twenty minutes later, I walked into the trendy restaurant where Macy had suggested we meet. The place was known for their upscale salads, soups, and sandwiches, although they did have entrée choices as well. The entire restaurant smelled like basil, freshly baked bread, and piles of money collecting in the register drawers.

Right away, I spotted Macy seated at a thick wooden table by the window. The woman was blonde and groomed to perfection. Her layered hair had perfect highlights, her makeup was thick but elegant, and she had jewelry on every place possible—except her nose and eyebrow. Her body showed she either had great genes or that she spent hours at the gym. My bets were on the gym.

If Brooke was anything like her friend, then she had expensive tastes, a high-maintenance lifestyle, and was perhaps a bit self-absorbed.

I know, I shouldn't judge a book by its cover . . . but I was doing it anyway. It was human nature, and, though that didn't make it right, a first impression was still a first impression.

I sat across from Macy and smiled. "Thanks for meeting with me."

"No problem." She set down her goblet of water and smiled back, though the action didn't quite reach her eyes. "I'm anxious to find out what happened to my friend as well."

Before I could dive into my questions, the waitress appeared. I ordered a salad and water . . . mostly out of guilt since that was what skinny Macy had ordered. I felt so non-cool with her—even if I'd only been with her for three minutes.

"How did you and Brooke know each other?" I started, dropping my knock-off purse on the floor.

"I'm a unit secretary in Labor and Delivery at the hospital."

"I see." I pulled out a pad of paper where I'd jotted some notes. "I'm trying to gather as much information as I can on what happened to Brooke. Maybe even make a timeline of what was going on in her life in the week or weeks before she disappeared."

I glanced at my notes, a list I'd scrawled together and that desperately needed help.

Thursday: unknown phone call

Monday: left for work at 7 a.m.

Weird phone call at lunch

Left work at 7 pm

Never returned home

Car found in parking garage by resort area oceanfront

I had a long way to go on this.

"I know it's not much," I said, staring at the skeleton list. "I'm just starting, and I'm meeting with Conrad later to fill in more. Can you help any?"

I noticed when I said Conrad's name that Macy rolled her eyes.

Before she could answer my question, I needed to call her out on her reaction. "You don't like Conrad?"

Macy shrugged, almost like she was trying to play off

her strong reaction, when, in truth, I knew she'd wanted me to see it. "It's complicated."

"Were Brooke and Conrad happy?"

"At times. I guess marriage is like that. Happy times. Not happy times. They were going through one of those not happy times . . . a rough patch."

I studied Macy a minute. No ring. No plans on a Sunday afternoon. No phone on the table in case anyone called. "Are you married?"

She let out a quick burst of laughter. "Me? No. Marriage isn't for me."

Those strong opinions just might be tainting her reaction to Conrad right now. She obviously wasn't a fan of settling down and all lifelong commitment brought with it.

"Why were Conrad and Brooke going through a rough patch?" I asked.

Macy tapped her manicured fingers against her water goblet. "Brooke wanted Conrad to get a different job. Being a teacher didn't bring in enough cash to sustain them."

"But she was a nurse, correct? So she brought in some income."

"That's the whole reason she went back to school to finish her degree. Conrad wasn't going to budge on the teaching thing, so Brooke had to make her own money in order to maintain her lifestyle."

Interesting. A possible source of resentment as well. "Was this an argument between them?"

"Oh, yeah. I mean, I didn't know her back before she became a nurse. But she was certainly bitter about having to work. And then, to add to it, she had student loans up to her eyeballs."

"Was Brooke just used to getting what she wanted?" I asked, trying to decide whether or not I liked Brooke. Right now, I was leaning toward not liking her. She sounded pretty materialistic and self-absorbed. That wasn't to say Conrad hadn't had his own issues and faults.

Our food came. My salad wasn't bad, but I really wanted the chicken parmesan the guy beside me was eating. At least Adele's pleasant tune through the overhead made me feel better and reminded me to "Set Fire to the Rain." Not when it came to salads, but when it came to living life and finding answers.

Macy dove right into her food, not even bothering to add salad dressing. "It's hard going from getting everything you want to barely being able to buy groceries. I mean, they live in this little house in the wrong part of town. She hated that. They drove old cars. And it was all because Conrad felt so passionate about being a teacher. He could have easily gotten a job again in engineering."

"What do you mean?" Another layer was being pulled back. Like an onion. Or like a house I'd helped restore once that had five different floors—carpet, vinyl, more vinyl, more vinyl, and finally beautiful hardwood. That job had taught me two things—layers were a lot of hard work, and they left me exhausted.

"I mean that when the two of them met, Conrad was an engineer. But he gave it all up when he heard his calling to the classroom."

It sounded noble enough. "I bet the transition was difficult."

"Especially when they couldn't have kids," Macy continued. "Brooke wanted in vitro, but they couldn't afford it."

I was getting a better picture of this marriage, and I didn't know whom to feel sorry for. It certainly didn't seem healthy. But marriage was hard work. And a lot of meeting in the middle. And a million different things that made it challenging yet wonderful.

Macy leaned closer. "I wasn't supposed to tell anyone, but Brooke actually got a second job and didn't tell Conrad."

"What?" This was the first I'd heard of that.

Macy nodded, like it was normal. "Yep. Brooke worked for a home health agency on the side. Hospice, actually. She . . . didn't handle it very well. Not everyone can do the end-of-life stuff. It's hard."

I knew what that was like—only I'd dealt with the end-of-life stuff after it happened. "How did she hide that from Conrad?"

"She told him she'd picked up some extra shifts at the

hospital, but she hadn't. Believe it or not, there weren't any openings there for her to get more hours."

"Why not just tell her husband?"

Macy shrugged and studied the cherry tomato she'd just stabbed with her fork. "I guess it was a matter of pride. She didn't want her husband to see how hard any of this was on her. She thought she'd work for a while until she got her debt paid off, and then life could resume as normal."

"I see."

Her eyelids drooped in snooty annoyance. "But I don't think this part-time job had anything to do with her disappearance. She quit."

"What was the name of this company?"

"I'm pretty sure it was Maranatha Health."

"I'll look into them. Anything else you want to share?"

She let out a small sigh. "There was this one man who made her uncomfortable at work. He seemed to be enamored with Brooke. He came in the first time with a cut on his arm, and he accidentally wandered up to the Labor and Delivery area. That was strange enough, but then he came back again a week later. This time, he brought her flowers. Brooke told him she was married, and he left."

"Do you have a name?" My pulse spiked. Maybe this was the lead we were looking for.

"No, he didn't give a name. All I remember is that he was tall and thin with dark hair. And it looked like half of his face had been burned in a fire."

"That's helpful." And I was surprised Detective Belfield hadn't mentioned that. "Did you tell the police?"

"I did send an anonymous email about it."

"Why anonymously?"

"I have a tendency not to trust police. My stepdad was a cop, and he was a royal jerk."

"That's terrible."

"It was. And I haven't been a fan of cops since. That's why I was thrilled when you called. Maybe you won't let me down."

I ate my last piece of overpriced lettuce. "This has been very helpful. Thank you, Macy."

I had some time to kill before meeting Conrad so, for fun, I swung by my old stomping grounds—a coffeehouse aptly named The Grounds.

As soon as I walked into the eclectic shop, the smell of cinnamon and coffee hit me, and I felt like I'd just hugged an old friend. Acoustic music played overhead—Ed Sheeran—and I figured if my current house didn't work out, I wouldn't mind living here instead.

My friend Sharon stood behind the counter, whipping up some addicting caffeinated creation. She smiled when she saw me and pulled out a cup, ready to make my drink without a word of instruction from me.

That was when you knew you had a good barista.

She'd just added some barstools near the counter area, so I slipped onto one of those and waited for the noise of the little frothing machine-y thingy to stop. As soon as Sharon handed the other customer her drink, she moseyed over to me.

"Good to see you, Gabby." She wiped her hands on a towel below the counter.

Seriously, baristas were like bartenders for people whose vice was caffeine instead of alcohol. I could sit here all day and tell her my problems. When I left, I'd be hyper instead of drunk. Seemed like a better bet to me.

"You too," I said.

"It's not the same without you across the street." Without me saying a word, she began fixing me a vanilla latte. She could read my mind like that.

But I frowned at her words, and my gaze slipped to the window. My old apartment complex used to regally stand across the street, like a Victorian lady looking over her quaint, urban territory. The old house had been cut up into five apartments and was nothing fancy.

But it had been home.

Until my brother had decided to build a meth lab in my apartment, and my whole building had gone up in flames.

He was now serving time in prison for the crime.

Sharon added a dollop of whipped cream on top of the cup in her hands and handed it to me. "Your dad's fiancé stopped by the other day. Teddi, right?"

"Yes, Teddi." The woman was good for my dad. Almost too good, which made me have mixed feelings. I mean, really, their relationship made me incredibly happy for my dad but unreasonably sad for Teddi. I wasn't sure the woman knew what she was getting into.

"Said the wedding day is getting closer."

"They keep trying to nail down a date," I said. "Hopefully, it will happen soon. They've been together for a while now."

"Working on a new case?"

I took a long sip of my drink, trying to wash away the acidic taste of the toxic police department brew. "Of course. Life would be boring without a reason to get nosy."

"What's this one about?"

I filled her in, and her eyes lit.

"Believe it or not, Brooke is a friend of a friend," Sharon said. "They did hot yoga together."

"Small world."

"You can say that again."

I leaned back. "What were your theories?"

Sharon shrugged and began wiping the counter as I took a sip of my drink. "Hard to say. I'm sure you've heard about Brooke and her husband and how different they were. My first thought is always that the husband is guilty. Nothing about this case has changed my mind."

"I see." Poor husbands—they always got a bad rap in

these cases. Unfortunately, most of the time they deserved it.

"I hope you can figure it out." Sharon paused long enough to fix a drink for another customer. "How are you and Riley doing, by the way? Now that you're all adulting and bought a house."

"We're good." I hoped my voice sounded as warm as I felt. We were good—but it had been a long road to get here.

"Next step is kids." Sharon raised her eyebrows.

If I had a quarter for every time I'd heard that . . . "Oh, I'm not sure if we're ready for kids yet."

"I don't think people are ever truly ready for kids. They just adjust when the kids come."

"Maybe. But Riley still needs time to reestablish himself in his law career, and I'm trying to figure out my future as well."

"Figure it out? I thought you were doing what you loved?" She stepped away to hand another customer a scone and a plain coffee.

"Well, I love working for Grayson Tech, but it is only part time. And I'm doing these cold cases on the side, but they're inconsistent. I'm not sure this is what I want to do for the rest of my life. Maybe it is." I hadn't meant to say all of that.

"What else would you do?"

I shrugged. I'd been thinking about my future a lot lately, but I hadn't reached any conclusions. It was just this niggling feeling in the back of my mind that kept catching my attention. "Go on full time with the police? Even working full time for Grayson might be nice."

"Then you couldn't do your cases on the side."

"True enough." I shrugged again. "I don't know. I just feel like there's more for me, and I'm trying to figure out what that more is. You know?"

"I hear you. I guess I'm lucky because I love this place." Sharon glanced around the coffee shop, a nook that was all the fruit of her labor. "It has its challenges, but I wouldn't change anything."

"Then you are lucky."

I wish I could say the same. I had no idea why I felt so contemplative lately. I had every reason to be happy, yet part of me wanted something more.

I was questioning my own sanity. I mean, I'd gone from a college dropout to a crime-scene cleaner, to getting my degree, still cleaning crime scenes, doing some official and unofficial PI work on the side, and now to working part time for Grayson Tech.

I suppose the driven side of me wanted more, though.

Yet I had nothing to complain about.

I finished my drink and paid before standing. "I have another meeting to get to."

"Good luck with your case."

"Thanks." Because it looked like I'd need it.

CHAPTER FOUR

*R*ight on time, I walked into the small gym that served as Riley's second home. The place wasn't anything fancy. It had previously served as a warehouse for an HVAC company. The place was still boxy with exposed ventilation on the ceiling. Handmade obstacles filled the room—a warp wall, balance beams, and others that I couldn't name, but they may have been torture devices in past centuries. All of the challenges had been arranged strategically on the floor.

Conrad and Riley seemed to spot me at the same time and came over to join me by the door. Riley kissed my cheek, sweat covering every visible surface of his skin. "Good to see you," he murmured.

"You too."

I was glad Riley had found something he loved doing

—something other than lawyering, which I knew wasn't really a word, but I liked it anyway.

I smiled at Conrad, who looked similar to Riley in matters of sweat. But unlike Riley—who had messy hair and the satisfied expression brought on by hard work—Conrad had perfect hair and shifty eyes.

And he looked tired. Exhausted, really.

"Thanks for meeting with me, Conrad," I started. "I won't take much of your time."

Riley nodded behind him. "I'm going to keep working out . . . unless you need me for anything."

I shook my head. "Nope. I'm good."

He kissed my cheek again and then jogged away. That was when I turned to Conrad, ready to have an uncomfortable talk. Before diving in, Conrad gave a bro nod to a man who entered. You know, the nod that guys gave each other, the one where they didn't have to say a word, but that one action somehow solidified comradery and support? It was pretty amazing, actually.

"So, you said you had some more questions for me?" Conrad started.

"I do." I shifted. "I talked to Macy Williamson today."

His gaze darkened. What was that reaction for? Macy had the same response when I'd mentioned Conrad's name.

"You don't like her?" I asked.

"She's fine. She liked to spend money just as much as

Brooke, so I didn't encourage their friendship. I think that made Macy resent me."

It made sense, I supposed. "Macy mentioned that you and Brooke fought quite a bit over finances."

"We did. But it wasn't over-the-top stuff. Just normal married couples' kind of stuff."

I'd be the judge of that. "You didn't tell me you'd changed jobs."

His lips twitched, like what I'd said had left a bad taste in his mouth. "I was miserable being an engineer. The money was good, but I had no satisfaction. I decided maybe I should teach instead. It was what I'd wanted to do, but my parents convinced me there was no future in being both a teacher and a provider for my family."

"You felt differently?"

"I figured that life was short, and that I should do what I loved. You learn to live within the confines of your finances. At least, smart people do."

I couldn't argue—although if he said that to Brooke in the same superior tone he'd said it to me, I could see where his wife might have bristled. "But Brooke didn't like that choice?"

"No. I mean, she agreed I could do it. Gave me her blessing. But once the money stopped coming in, I could tell she wasn't happy. When she decided to go back and get her degree in nursing, I thought that might be the best thing for us all around. It would give her not only money, but something to do with her time other than shopping and going to the spa and expensive girls' nights."

"Did it work?"

"Not really. Shopping is addictive. You can never have enough. At least, that's how it seemed. Brooke got online and kept finding things she needed. She wasn't satisfied."

"And so she got a part-time job?"

His face darkened again. "That's right. And she didn't tell me about it until I discovered her debt. She'd told me she was getting overtime at the hospital instead."

So he had known about it. Why hadn't Conrad mentioned it to me earlier? Something was weird about this part-time job. "Why did she do that?"

"We'd had a big fight a few months earlier, and I threatened to leave. It was the only thing I could think of to help get our finances under control—to give her an ulti-matum. This was before I knew about her secret credit cards. And it seemed to work. Brooke freaked out. She didn't want to separate. But then she went and found this job and hid it from me."

"Why would she do that? Why not just get a part-time job and tell you about it?"

"I have no idea. I almost got a part-time job myself, just to pay down some of our debt. But I figured she was the one who'd racked up thousands of dollars. It made more sense if she was the one who had to work a little harder to pay it off. She's been handed things her entire life."

"I see." I wasn't sure if that made him smart or a jerk.

"We wanted to try in vitro as well. And that's really costly. She wanted her parents to pay for it, but I said we should pay for it ourselves."

It sounded like Conrad had a lot of opinions. And they weren't all wrong or bad. But they were strong, and again I wondered just what his and Brooke's interactions at home were like.

"Did you catch her working this second job?"

"I did. I stopped by the hospital to surprise her with lunch, but she wasn't there. The charge nurse looked at me like I was crazy and said that Brooke never worked weekends. I decided not to confront Brooke, though. Instead, the next day I followed her."

"And?" This case was juicier than I'd imagined it might be.

"She pulled up to a house. I thought for sure I was going to catch her having an affair. I waited, trying to gather my thoughts. Then I saw her walk outside with an elderly woman who was crying. The homeowner's name was on the mailbox, so I did a little research. It led me back to this person's social media profile, and I realized the man who lived in the home was dying."

"Did you confront her?"

He grabbed a towel from a community stack near the check-in desk and rubbed the white terrycloth across his face. Was he sweating because it was hot in here? Or because his heart rate had elevated due to guilt?

"No, I didn't," he said. "Actually, I started feeling bad. I saw that I'd been a little too harsh in my stance and that Brooke was miserable as a result. I knew that line of nursing wasn't what she wanted. She was always so compassionate and sensitive. She lost one patient once in the hospital—and she cried for a week."

"I would imagine that would be difficult."

He nodded stiffly. "When Brooke came home that evening, I told her I was going to be doing some tutoring after school. I was also considering going back into engineering."

I blinked at his words. "Really?"

"Was my happiness worth sacrificing my wife's happiness? I'm still not sure what the right answer is. But I didn't want to see her struggling. I figured going into engineering would be the best thing for our marriage."

"But you're still teaching?"

"I told Brooke that, and she broke down. Said I shouldn't have to do that. That I just needed to give her some time to pay off her debt and then she'd behave. We could put away some money and maybe do in vitro—when we were sure we had the cash."

"It sounds like you were working things out then."

"Except a week later she disappeared. Which made it even harder. I mean, I thought we were on the same page. I thought we'd gotten past our hard times. I guess I was wrong."

I shifted, wishing this place wasn't so loud. And hot.

And non-private. "I always have to ask this, Conrad. And I know it's not an easy question."

"She wasn't having an affair." He narrowed his eyes, looking annoyed, and reading my mind.

"You've obviously heard the question before."

"The police harped on it. But there weren't any signs there. I just can't believe Brooke would do something like that."

"She was in contact with her ex."

Conrad shrugged. "They remained friends after their breakup, but it was never anything inappropriate. Besides, he was out of town when all of this happened, and the police cleared him."

I wish I could be that sure. "Did the police check her laptop?"

"Some. I mean, they didn't take it. But I think they looked at her emails."

I wanted to see those emails. And maybe talk to her ex even. And her parents. "I have a friend coming into town, and he's a computer forensic guy. Top notch. Would you mind if we took a look at it?"

"Not at all. In fact, I'll give you a key to my place. Go in. Look at anything and everything. I have nothing to hide."

I leaned closer. "Are you sure you're prepared for what we might find? It might not be what you want."

His face remained stoic. "I just want answers, whatever those answers are."

Riley had left the gym earlier so he could run home and return a couple phone calls for work. Meanwhile, I'd grabbed some Chinese takeout. I looked forward to talking things through with Riley back at the house.

Armed with a bag of General Tso's chicken, I went inside and dropped my keys on the dining room card table. I paused for a minute, sucking in a deep, long breath. Everything was quiet.

Which was weird.

Where was Riley? He usually greeted me at the door if he was here when I arrived. And, according to his car outside and our previous conversation, he should be home.

Noise from my backyard caught my ear. I stepped outside and saw Riley, Sierra, Chad, and Reef standing in a circle.

I paused at the edge of the group. If the day had been warm or sunny, I might guess they were enjoying the weather. But it was overcast, and the wind made it chilly enough for a coat and maybe even a scarf.

Before I could say anything, a flash of brown and black fur flew past, chasing a ball, turning circles, and then running away again.

Everyone chuckled, like this was entertaining enough that they'd be willing to pay twenty dollars a ticket plus ten bucks in sneaky surcharges to watch it.

"What in the world?" I said.

Finally, everyone noticed me. Riley stepped back toward me and kissed my cheek. "Sorry. I didn't hear you come home."

I hardly heard him. I was watching the dog. In my yard. With my people.

Not the dog's people. *Mine.*

"Who is this?' I finally asked, my throat questionably tight.

"We don't know his name." Sierra's eyes were fixated on the dog. "He showed up at your door but doesn't have any tags."

Chad threw a ball, and the dog chased it across the yard again.

"Is he okay?" I asked. "Maybe a stray?"

"He's a little skinny, but I gave him some rice and gravy. He perked right up."

"He just showed up here at my door?" I verified. A dog had never just shown up at my door. Then I remembered Lucky, the parrot that had been stuck in a tree outside my apartment on the night Riley and I first met. Maybe stray animals were just drawn to us.

We still had Lucky to this day. He'd taken up residence in the back bedroom—now Riley's office—in a corner by the window.

"Yeah, the pooch was on the porch when I got home," Riley said. "I thought Sierra had brought him here."

The dog ran up to me and dropped the ball at my feet

before panting happily. He sat there until I patted his head, and then he leaned into the action like any affection was an absolute treat.

"What kind of dog is this?" I'd guess the canine to be about fifty pounds, maybe a year old. His body was a reddish-tan color, but his face and ears had black markings. His snout was long, his feet and chest white, and his ears showed he was perky and alert.

"I think he's a German shepherd mix," Sierra said. "Maybe with a basenji."

"A what?" Riley asked.

"They're these great dogs from central Africa," Sierra said. "They're scrappy and smart. Also endearing and great companions. I mean, just look at the wrinkle across his brow. Have you ever seen something so cute or inquisitive?"

I leaned down to meet the dog's gaze. "I'm sorry you wandered away from home, boy. What are you going to do now? Do you have a friend down the street you can stay with? Maybe a lady friend? I'm not suggesting you shack up. There are respectable ways of doing things, you know."

"Oh, Gabby." Sierra chuckled. "I guess we can put up signs around the neighborhood saying we found him."

"And then he'll stay with you until someone claims him?" I clarified.

Sierra's eyebrows shot up. "With me? And my cats? And Reef? Wow. I'd love to. You know I would. But, as much I love that guesthouse, it's not big enough for all of us."

I was getting a bad feeling about this. "So where will he go?"

"I hate to say it, but I guess I could take him to a no-kill shelter." Sierra frowned, and her entire face went pale, almost as if she'd just been told Chad was going to prison for life.

The dog continued to stare at me, waiting for my response. "A shelter? I thought you hated those places."

The putrid look remained on her face. "You're right. I should find a foster home . . . except every rescue group I know is strapped for volunteers right now. Do you know of anyone willing to foster?"

"Foster a dog?" I stared at the canine and shrugged. The people I interacted with chased down criminals with hopes of putting them away. We didn't exactly talk about taking in strays so they wouldn't end up behind bars. "I mean . . . no. I've never asked."

"He could stay with us until we either find his owners or a foster home, right?" Riley looked over at me, and his expression matched the dog's—puppy dog eyes and all.

Did Riley like this dog? Was my husband a dog person? This was . . . unexpected.

"I guess. I mean, I don't see why not." I couldn't think of one solid excuse that wouldn't make me sound like a jerk.

"Great." Riley squatted and rubbed the dog's head. "We'll take care of you, boy."

The dog licked Riley's face, and Riley smiled like a kid at Christmas.

This was not how I envisioned my day ending.

CHAPTER FIVE

An hour later, Riley and I had found some old pillows that would serve as the dog's bed, some old bowls the dog could use for food and water, and we'd given the beast a bath. Meanwhile, Sierra had made some posters, and she and her family were walking around the neighborhood and hanging them on telephone poles. She'd started outside my place, probably to make sure I saw her.

"We've got to give him a name." Riley sat in his chair and stared at the dog. The dog stared back, equally as smitten with Riley. "Even if it's just temporary."

Naming him sounded like a bad, bad idea. Despite that, I asked, "What do you think?"

"Hmm . . ." He studied the dog's face. "Bandit?"

"Bandit should definitely be in the running." The

dog's pointy ears, inquisitive eyes, and friendly disposition seemed to fit the name.

"How about something that fits you as an investigator? Something like Sherlock?"

"Now you're thinking like me. But this dog doesn't strike me as a Sherlock. He's more of a Watson."

I mentally told myself that I hadn't said that because I was thinking of the dog as a sidekick. It was purely just an observation with absolutely no bearing on my future.

"That's a good one also. I like it."

"How about Sir Watson?" It had a better ring to it, and I really needed to stop this insanity.

Riley rubbed the dog's head. "That's it. Sir Watson."

Sir Watson barked in approval, the sound deep and excited.

"You do know this is just temporary, right?" I reminded Riley, hating to be a killjoy. But someone had to be that person, and it wasn't Riley.

"Oh, yeah. Of course." He rubbed Sir Watson's head with both of his hands and made a baby face at the canine.

Riley said he understood, but I could see my sweet husband getting attached. It reminded me to keep my distance. The dog was only temporary, and getting attached to him would just mean sadness in the end.

I tried to stop staring at the dog and turned to Riley instead. "We haven't really had a chance to talk."

"No, we haven't. How's the case going? And when is

the rest of the crew coming into town?" He leaned back. Sir Watson tried to jump up onto the couch and sit beside Riley, but I shooed the dog down. He plopped on the floor instead.

"They're flying in tomorrow."

"Staying here?" Weariness etched his voice.

"No, they're getting two rooms at the Burwood Hotel in Norfolk. I thought it would be better if we all had some space."

"Especially considering that we haven't finished unpacking."

I frowned as I looked at the boxes lining the room. "We've really got to get on that, don't we?"

"Yeah, we do." Riley put his arm around me and pulled me toward him. "Next weekend. If you're done with the case. That's all we'll do. Just take a few days to get this place together and make it our own. We can actually paint these walls, you know."

"I know. No more white walls of rental-dom." That sounded amazing.

"Exactly."

"And this used furniture was donated. We can use what we want but buy new stuff and re-donate the rest." People had stepped in to help us after the fire. We'd lost pretty much everything. For example, the couch we sat on right now? While in good condition, it was mauve and floral. Not at all my taste, though I was grateful for the gift.

"I kind of miss our apartment," I muttered.

"I know. I do too. There were a lot of memories there."

"Almost all of our memories were there." Meeting Riley. Solving cases. Defusing bombs. Almost getting killed.

"The good news is that memories are something we hold in our minds and hearts. Nothing can take that away."

I pulled my head back and looked Riley in the eye. "I like that. A lot."

His eyes twinkled. "You know what I like a lot?"

"What?"

"You." His lips covered mine.

Which was good. Because I liked him too.

Bright and early the next morning, Evie and Sherman flew in from Texas and Kansas, respectively. They'd decided to pick up a rental car together—it was better to have more than one vehicle in these investigations—and they met me at my place.

Part of me felt like I should run from my porch and throw my arms around them like long-lost friends when they pulled up. But Evie wasn't the huggy, warm type of gal. And Sherman was usually so focused on Evie, that he wouldn't care if I greeted him with a hug or not.

So, instead, I casually made my way down the sidewalk and plastered on a bright grin. "Look who pulled into town."

"Is that a nicer way of saying look what the cat dragged in?" Evie said, climbing from the driver's seat.

Well, hello to you too.

I ignored her biting comment and smiled again. "Nope. Not at all. I'm so glad you guys are here. Come inside so we can talk."

Evie paused for a moment and stared at my house with her assessing, slightly judgmental gaze. The woman hadn't changed since I'd seen her last. She wore black slacks and a white shirt that seemed to match her dark hair and pale skin. Evie was thin, and, just like everything else in her life, the way she looked and dressed was purposeful and neat and no-nonsense.

"I have only six days until I have to be back," Evie said. "I think it will be better if we skip the chitchat and jump right into this case. I reviewed everything you sent me while on the plane."

I exchanged a glance with Sherman, who shrugged like he wanted to not like Evie's approach, but he was unable to commit to fully disliking it because he was so enamored with the woman. Poor guy.

"Sure thing," I said. "Let's go inside."

As soon as we stepped through the front door, Sir Watson bounded over. And his sights were set on Evie.

Of course.

Evie's eyes widened as if she was horrified or terrified

or maybe both. The next moment, the dog's paws were on her shoulders, and Sir Watson licked her face, despite her screams of protest. Or maybe because of them.

"Sir Watson, down!" I ordered, as if every dog would instantly know that command.

"What. Is. This? I didn't know you had a dog. Couldn't we have met somewhere else?" It was like someone had thrown slime on Evie or something.

Nope, she wasn't happy.

"Sir Watson needs a place to stay until we find his owners." I took the dog's collar and pulled him down, giving a warning look that did absolutely no good. The canine's eyes were still bright, playful, and satisfied. "Let me just get him a bone."

I was new at this whole dog ownership—albeit temporary—thing. But I fished some kind of rawhide thing from a bag of treats Riley had picked up and handed the treat to the dog. He took it and went to his dog pillows in the corner to chew.

The dog had done surprisingly well last night. He'd lain on the floor beside my bed and had only awakened us once. And, as much as I wanted to be upset, Sir Watson had only stirred because a car outside had backfired. At least he'd had a good reason.

I offered a weak smile to my friends. "Have a seat. I'm sure you're tired from your flight."

"The act of moving through distance so quickly and at such a high elevation does take a toll on the body," Evie said, lowering herself onto the couch—after briefly turning up her nose at it.

I glanced at Sherman again. At the blue shirt he wore with a cartoon cat sticking out of the front pocket. His jeans—the kind that weren't trendy and weren't even a style. At his short dark hair—hair so thick most men dreamed about it. At his glasses, which were a constant source of movement for him. He was always shoving them up higher on his nose, probably as more of a nervous habit than because he actually needed to.

"How was your trip?" I asked him.

As if on cue, he pushed his glasses up higher. "I can't complain."

That was what I liked to hear. No complaints or drama. Only happiness.

I pointed to his shirt. "Nice frocket."

He blinked. "What?"

"You know, front pocket mashed together as one word —frocket. Life is more fun when people invent new words."

He glanced down at his shirt. "Oh, uh . . . thank you."

"Let me get you some coffee," I said.

Before anyone could stop me, I went into my kitchen and brought out a tray I'd prepared just for them. I set it on the coffee table, ignoring my instincts for rambling small talk. Evie had already made it clear my thoughts on the weather, *The Greatest Showman*, and the price of eggs weren't welcome.

"Tell us what you know." Evie daintily poured her coffee, stirred in some sugar, and leaned back.

I took a deep breath before launching into everything I'd learned.

Evie's eyebrows flickered up as I finished. "The husband did it."

I cocked my head to the side, feeling a little bad for Conrad since everyone automatically assumed his guilt. "I know that's often the case, but we should keep an open mind. He seemed nice enough."

"Nice guys are capable of murder," she continued.

"I suppose everyone is capable of murder," I said. "But I'd like to look at every angle of this case."

"Of course." She snorted, like I was the one who'd jumped to conclusions.

I suddenly remembered how difficult Evie had been to work with on our last case. In fact, I may have vowed to never work with her again. But then we'd kind of made up, and I'd blamed her persnickety attitude on her having a hard life.

And Sherman would never be on my side if I ditched her because he was too smitten with Evie.

I'd loved the thought of this cold-case squad when Garrett Mercer had come to me with the idea. The execution was always a little more difficult than the ideal.

Sherman pushed his glasses up higher on his nose again and raised his coffee. "Where do you think we should start, Gabby?"

"Conrad—the husband—has given us permission to go into his house and look at whatever we need, including his wife's computer. I think it's a good idea. We can get a better feel for her and their marriage."

"And him," Evie added.

"And him."

She stood. "Let's go then. Do you have a to-go mug for this coffee? And please say that dog is not coming with us."

I needed a happy soundtrack to begin playing in my life right now. But I could already feel myself getting cranky. And we were only just starting this.

Never. A. Good. Sign.

CHAPTER SIX

Conrad had given me a spare key to his place. Still, part of me felt guilty going into the house without him there. Then again, this had been his idea and not mine.

"Not bad digs for a teacher." Evie looked around the small bungalow.

I'd expected far worse after talking to Macy. This place didn't look terrible at all or like it was in a horrible part of town. Sure, they were small houses—similar to my own—in an older neighborhood.

Maybe to Brooke and Macy this area was too lowbrow. But it didn't look bad to me. However, I hadn't grown up wealthy or privileged.

"I heard Brooke had good taste." And by looking at her house, I'd agree. It was decorated like someone with an eye for fashion and style had taken the reins.

Which was what I could only assume had happened.

Everything was farmhouse style with distressed wood furniture, a barn door near the dining room, and dried flowers in a milk jug on a shelf near the front door. The place even smelled like cotton and sunflowers.

How much debt had Brooke racked up making this place look like it could have been on *Fixer Upper*? I had no doubt that no expense had been spared.

"What are we looking for?" Evie stood in the entry with her hands on her hips.

"That's the question. Anything that gives us insight into Brooke and what happened."

"Where is her computer?" Sherman asked.

"Conrad said it was the laptop in the office." I glanced at my phone, where I'd taken some notes. "He even gave me the password. A sure sign he's not guilty."

I flashed a quick look at Evie, watching her expression.

She scowled at me, as expected.

"I'll look at the bedroom," she said.

"And I'll take the living room."

I didn't expect to find much. Even if Conrad was somehow behind this, he would be smart enough to hide anything important before inviting us in.

Most likely.

I had worked with my fair share of not-so-smart criminals. People were criminals for a reason—mostly because they tried to take the easy way instead of using their brains to obtain what they wanted the legal way.

I paced around the neat space, figuring it had probably looked even neater and more well-polished when Brooke was here. Right now, there was a coffee mug still on the end table. Dust added a layer of gray to the TV stand. A blanket was strewn on the couch, and a basket of clothes waited to be folded by the recliner.

It was a change from the OCD tendencies I'd seen in the man at the restaurant. Perhaps he only got meticulous about details when he was nervous. Or maybe he tried not to spend too much time here—too many memories— and as a result, his house wasn't spick-and-span.

I stopped by a picture of Conrad and Brooke on the end table. They smiled for the camera, their arms wrapped around each other, and a blue sky met green mountain as the two blurred in the background.

They looked like any other happy couple. The photo could have been Riley and me. The two just looked so normal.

I knew that not every photo was a snapshot of life. Maybe of life at that very moment. But moments could cover up the other 99 percent of reality.

Were these two really happy? I didn't know.

"I don't see anything on this computer that would indicate Brooke was engaged in a secret life," Sherman announced.

I crossed the house to join him in the office.

"I was able to quickly look at her emails, her deleted emails, and her social media accounts. I also went into a section of the computer containing deleted files, and I checked to see if she had any of those programs that erases messages five minutes after they're sent. I didn't see any evidence of that."

I stood behind him and sighed. "Well, at least we know."

"I'm sure the police have already gone through her text messages, and you said they shared that information with you."

"Correct," I said. It had been in the case file.

Sherman shrugged. "So I'm not sure we've learned anything new."

"Except maybe that Brooke was faithful." And that was something important.

Evie came down the hallway. She'd obviously heard our conversation. "Check *his* computer."

Wow, she really was intent on the fact that Conrad was the bad guy here. Maybe it had something to do with the fact that her foster dad had left her foster mom for another woman. In her mind, had that act made every man a dog?

Sherman looked up at me. "What do you think?"

I hesitated. "Conrad did say we could look wherever we wanted. I suppose it couldn't hurt."

Sherman twisted the chair back toward the computer. "I'm on it."

I continued to wander through Conrad's house. I opened his fridge. Saw a good selection of healthy fruits and vegetables, and an impressive collection of fluorescent-colored energy drinks.

I looked through his stack of mail. Again, it was just the normal—nothing that told me anything of importance.

I even stepped into his backyard. I knew it was a long shot, but I decided to search the property there for any soil that had been disturbed. And, of course, there was nothing.

"Can I help you?" a neighbor across the waist-high fence asked. He was an older man with a white mustache and severely receding hairline. He held a bottle in his hand with a spray nozzle in the end.

Weeds, I realized. The man was spraying weeds.

Did people do that in the winter? I had no idea. I wasn't a gardener, but I knew that people who loved their plants fiddled with them as often as possible.

His backyard was immaculate, filled with various kinds of birdhouses and birdfeeders, a koi pond with a waterfall, and a lovely gazebo in the corner.

"We're here with permission from Conrad," I said. "He's hired us to investigate his wife's disappearance."

"Poor Brooke." The man frowned and paused from his work. "I was devastated to hear she'd disappeared. I still pray for her every night—pray that she's okay."

"What do you think happened?"

"I really don't know," the man said. "I know she and

her husband did fight some. But I also know they looked at each other with that look—the one that said they loved each other."

That was good to know. "So you don't think things got violent between them?"

He let out a quick breath of air and set his weed killer on the grass. "Oh, no. Not at all. How could anyone ever hurt Brooke? She was kind and sweet."

Maybe Brooke was different from the picture I'd formed in my mind. "I'm glad to hear she was a good person."

"I can't imagine her getting mixed up in anything shady," he said. "I mean, she even brought me dinner for a week after my wife died. Would a criminal do that?"

I didn't want to tell him yes, but I'd seen it all. Still, the picture he'd painted was of someone with a good heart. He needed to hold on to that for as long as possible.

He picked up his weed killer again but made no effort to begin working. "Another thing I thought was weird—I saw someone going through their mail three different times."

My muscles clenched with curiosity. "What?"

He nodded. "I told the police. They didn't seem to think anything of it."

"When was this? Before Brooke disappeared?"

"Yes, probably about a month before. I tried to confront the man once, but he jumped in his car and pulled away."

"What did this man look like?"

"He did have one distinguishing mark. It was a scar across the entire left side of his face."

A scar? Did that match up with the information Macy had shared about the man who'd harassed Brooke at the hospital? She'd said half of his face looked like it had been burned.

I kept those facts in the back of my mind.

"Thank you for your help," I told the neighbor. "We're going to do our best to find Brooke."

"I hope you do. And I hope she's okay."

I walked slowly back into the house, my shoes crunching against the dry grass beneath them. I'd really hoped we might discover some kind of clue here, but we hadn't.

Would this be the case that I couldn't solve?

It had to happen sometime. Yet I could hardly stomach the thought of my first loss.

As soon as I walked in, I heard Sherman say, "Gabby, Evie, look at this."

Evie and I went over to the desktop computer where he sat. Some type of website was up on the screen.

"What are we looking at?" Evie asked.

Sherman tapped a few more keys before releasing the keyboard and leaning back. "You know those hidden social media sites that delete your messages after you send them?"

"I've heard of them." Never used them, thank goodness. How people juggled so much deceit was beyond me. I could barely keep up with the truth.

"Well, our faithful husband Conrad has one of those sites," Sherman continued. "Most people wouldn't be able to retrieve the messages from them, but thanks to my extensive training—and mostly just my God-given smarts —I was able to pull some of the messages up."

"What did they say?" I could hardly breathe as I asked the question.

Sherman looked at us, satisfaction in his gaze. "Let's just say that Conrad has been talking to a woman. Someone who even asked him to meet her. And the details sound intimate."

CHAPTER SEVEN

I read and reread the hidden emails between Conrad and a woman named Emily No-Last-Name so many times that my eyes began to hurt. I didn't want to believe what I saw. But there was no denying it.

These emails were like a blazing confirmation that Conrad was not the perfect husband.

You were the best kisser ever, Conrad said.

Life would be different if we were together, Emily replied. *Maybe it's time to move on.*

Dinner was amazing, Conrad wrote. *Thank you for everything.*

"He's having an affair," Evie said with an assertive nod of her head. "He killed off his wife so he could be with this Emily woman. Case solved."

"Why wouldn't he just get divorced?" Even as I said

the words, I knew the truth. I just needed to hear it from someone else.

"Because then his ex takes half of his money, and this guy hardly has any money to begin with." Evie said the words like she was explaining first grade math to a college senior. "There's stigma. If his wife disappears tragically, he gets sympathy. He gets the limelight. The psychological profile of someone like this is vast and fascinating."

"And the fact that he hid the emails through this program only further indicates that he's guilty of something." Sherman twirled his thumbs, almost as an outward sign of his inner processor.

"When are these messages dated?" I propped my hip against the wall in thought. I didn't want to believe it. I was rooting for Conrad and Brooke's marriage. For faithfulness. For love that would be everlasting, just like Nat King Cole had sung about.

Sherman leaned toward the computer and squinted. "They started . . . two months ago."

"So maybe their relationship started after Brooke disappeared." I wasn't sure that was any better or less of a guilt indicator, but it could be worse. The emails could have started six months ago.

"Conrad could have been texting this woman on a burner phone before he discovered this program, which would have been a blazing red flag," Sherman said. "Or maybe he wasn't. We really don't know, do we?"

I released the air I'd been holding in my lungs. We didn't know, and it would be nearly impossible to find out if they had utilized something like a burner phone. "I'll look into it. I'll ask Conrad and try to feel him out."

"Because you think someone like this will tell you the truth?" Evie snorted. "No, you need to talk to Emily."

I pushed aside my irritation. "Emily has no last name. So how am I going to talk to her?"

"I can help." Sherman typed a few things into the computer before leaning back. "And there we have it. Emily Hayman. It looks like she lives an hour from here. I say we pay her a visit."

"Sounds good. Let's see if we can find some answers." I glanced at my watch. "But first I need to stop at home for a moment and check on Sir Watson."

Evie rolled her eyes.

I shrugged, trying not to let her get to me. "Riley's in court, so he can't do it."

I hadn't planned on becoming a dog owner. No, not owner. A dog *sitter*. A doggy foster mom? Whatever the term was, I was still adjusting.

This little detour should only take a minute, and then we'd be back on track to investigating. In theory, at least.

I dropped Sherman and Evie off at their car. They were going to check into their hotel and then meet me at my place in thirty. It would be nice to have a moment alone.

Or, should I say, alone with Sir Watson. I'd left him in my laundry room—all my supplies safely put away so he wouldn't be injured. I'd even cracked the window a little bit so he could have some fresh air.

But when I walked into my house, I paused. My house. My *new* house. The one I hadn't lived in for long enough to add my own nicks to the countertops or scrapes on the wall or kicks in the door.

There was cotton everywhere. Like it had snowed.

Inside.

In March.

Everywhere.

And Sir Watson sat at my feet, tongue hanging out, and telltale puffs of white on the corners of his mouth.

"How did you . . . ? What . . . ?" I glanced over and saw my couch. The floral, mauve one. The cushions had been completely destroyed. Demolished. Strewn about like Edward Scissorhands had personally seen to redecorating the space.

I looked back at Sir Watson. He wagged his tail at me.

In all honesty, the dog looked so adorable I wanted to rub his head and make duck lips. But I couldn't reward him for . . . for whatever this was.

"What have you done?" I muttered.

Sir Watson barked in return.

Someone knocked at the door behind me, and I turned to see Sierra and Reef standing there. Sierra had been working at home lately, unable to bring herself to take Reef to daycare. She did have a sitter come for a couple days a week so she could go into the office at the animal rights organization she ran.

"Wow." Sierra paused, my canine-loving friend even looking shocked. "I'm not going to ask."

"I put him in the laundry room." As I said the words aloud, I realized I needed to check out the space. This dog wasn't Houdini. How had he gotten out?

I walked through the kitchen and saw the laundry room door beyond it was open. I peered inside and saw that everything inside was just as I'd left it.

Maybe the dog *was* Houdini.

"He probably pawed the handle and opened the door," Sierra said.

I glanced at the handle. It was the old-fashioned kind with an arm on it instead of a knob. I suppose if Sir Watson's paw had hit that, the latch would have released.

"You're too smart for your own good," I told the dog.

He panted some more.

I turned away from the dog and back to my friend. I really didn't have time for this right now. "Anyone call yet to claim him?"

Sierra frowned. "It's been radio silent. Nothing. No one. I'm sorry."

"I never liked that couch anyway."

"It was hideous. But I'll get you a crate. At least he won't tear up anything else."

"I was hoping his owner would claim him before we spent too much money." Riley and I had just bought this house, and we were adjusting to the higher bills we had as a result. We were trying to stick to a budget, which was easier for Riley than it was me.

I glanced back at the dog, wondering what I'd gotten myself into.

If Brooke could mysteriously disappear without a trace, maybe Sir Watson could also.

I frowned at the thought. Because, even though I hadn't said a word out loud, I knew in my silent thoughts that I was bluffing.

I wouldn't forgive myself if this dog ended up in a hopeless situation.

was silent as Evie drove to Emporia, a town about an hour and a half away from Norfolk, and the place that Emily Hayman called home.

All I could think about was Sir Watson, my brand-new tarnished house, and how I really wanted some coffee from The Grounds to make this all better.

Evie was talking about some kind of conference she'd gone to last month, and Sherman was listening fully and completely. Then again, Sherman would listen fully and completely to anything Evie had to say, even if it was about the best way to pick spinach out of your teeth.

And Sir Watson sat beside me.

Yes, beside me.

Evie was driving my car.

And I couldn't stand the thought of leaving Sir Watson alone. Not because I loved him so much. No, because I couldn't stand the thought of what other kinds of damage he might do while I was gone.

But the flipside of that equation was that my window was cracked, tufts of fur raced around in the air, and the distinct smell of canine lingered around me. The radio murmured in the background.

I turned my ear toward the speaker. Was that "Who Let the Dogs Out?"

Yes, the perfect soundtrack to my life always seemed to be present, like God Himself knew I needed the perfect music to solidify the precarious situations I got myself into.

My mind wandered back to the conversation when I heard Evie say, "Men just weren't programmed to be faithful."

I couldn't just let that declaration slip by. Evie had said it as an absolute when it absolutely wasn't.

"You can't make a blanket statement like that," I argued.

"But it's true. We try to make humans penguins when in fact they're like rabbits. Rabbits are actually one of the most promiscuous—"

I raised a hand to silence her. "I get it. I really don't need to know any details on the escapades of rabbits."

Evie had been hanging around Sierra too long. Except she hadn't. But maybe they *should* hang out since Sierra was the queen of animal references.

"There are plenty of faithful men out there," I told her, glancing at my wedding ring.

"But their instinct is to cheat. To conquer. To dominate." Evie's voice was solid, leaving no room for argument.

I rolled my eyes and argued anyway. "I think you're overstating it."

"And I think marriage and monogamy are overblown."

Was there any hope for my friend? I wasn't sure.

And if there was no hope for Evie, that meant there was no hope for Sherman because Sherman was so obviously in love with the woman.

I pressed my lips together. When Garrett Mercer had first asked me to put this team together, I'd envisioned us being something like the team from *Criminal Minds* or *Law and Order*: one cohesive unit that didn't always see eye to eye, but whose differences only made them stronger. But really I was feeling more like we should star in our own episode of Jerry Springer.

"I just looked up some more information on this Emily woman," Sherman said, staring at his laptop. Perhaps he'd been trying to block out this conversation. I wouldn't blame him. "Emily Hayman is twenty-seven years old, and she got divorced last year. It appears she was married for seven years."

"Married at twenty?" Evie said. "That's way too young."

Her commentary could stop any time now.

"Keep going," I told Sherman. Sir Watson lay down on the seat beside me and put his chin on my lap. Against my better judgment, I patted his head.

"She's a teacher also, it appears," he said.

"Suspicious," Evie muttered.

"No children. Her social media profiles make her seem quite different than Brooke," Sherman said.

"How so?" I leaned forward just enough to hear but not far enough that Sir Watson had to move. Why was I accommodating the dog? I wasn't sure.

"Well, if you look at Brooke's social media, you'll see she's pretty gregarious," Sherman said. "She's always smiling, always surrounded by people, always at events around town. Emily, on the other hand, has pictures of herself with books. She posts her favorite recipes. She talks about liking time at home by herself."

"Introvert versus extrovert," Evie said.

"When you consider the problems Brooke and Conrad were having, maybe it was refreshing to connect with someone who was different than Brooke," I said before catching myself. I almost sounded like I was justifying it, which was the last thing I wanted to do. "Then again, maybe we're jumping to a lot of conclusions here. Maybe we should just wait and talk to Emily."

Sir Watson nuzzled my hand in agreement.

"I thought this was a three-person team," Evie muttered. "It sounds like you want to call all the shots."

Maybe this cold-case squad was a bad idea. Maybe this should be our last case, and I should be done with it.

I wasn't sure.

But Sir Watson was looking more and more tempting as a sidekick.

We got to Emily's house at 3:30. And, of course, she wasn't there.

So we parked my car near her house, and I walked Sir Watson for a little while and gave him some water—I'd brought it with me, along with a bowl and some plastic grocery bags.

Emily's neighborhood was nice but unremarkable. The homes here were probably thirty years old—little brick ranches, probably 1,400 square feet in size, which was small compared to all the new homes being built in the area. The community didn't appear to have a housing association, because some yards were well manicured while others had multiple cars parked out front—and not on the driveway—along with sprouts of weeds, crooked mailboxes, and even a few chain-link fences.

Emily's house fell into the first category. It wasn't extravagant, but she did have a neat rocker painted a coral color on the porch. Her door was a pleasant shade of lemonade yellow. And a wreath on the door had been embellished with happy-looking wooden letters reading, Hello!

When I got back to the car, Evie decided she would take a turn at stretching her legs as we waited.

After she left, I leaned forward, ready to talk to Sherman for a moment in private. "Did you tell Evie you like her yet?"

Sherman's eyes widened, and he pushed his glasses up higher as his cheeks turned as red as an "Off" button. "What? Evie? Me? No."

"I thought you were going to tell her." We'd had this conversation before.

"I can't do that. I haven't even talked to her in . . ."

"In how long?" I asked, leaning on the seat so I could read more of his expression.

Sherman shrugged, not saying anything for a moment. He stared out the window at Evie. "Since we were all together last time."

"What?" My voice screeched up higher. "Why not?"

"She fascinates me . . . and terrifies me."

I couldn't really argue with that. Evie was pretty scary. But . . . "I thought you liked her."

"I do like her. But you heard her. I don't think Evie's ready for any type of relationship."

That was the persona she'd created, at least. "She's just scared."

"And that equals not ready." His gaze was still on Evie, who was walking along as if involved in a funeral procession. Her steps were slow, her face solemn, and I could almost hear the sad music playing around her.

I sighed and didn't know what else to say. It was just as well because Evie climbed back in the car a few seconds later. Just as she did, a subcompact SUV pulled into the driveway of the house we were watching. A woman who looked like Emily stepped out, dressed in khakis and a sweater, flinging a tote bag over her shoulder.

"This is it, guys," I muttered. "Showtime."

Wasting no more time, we all climbed out. I cracked the windows to leave Sir Watson inside and prayed that he would behave.

I didn't have much hope of that happening. But I had no other choice right now, unless I wanted to wait in the car. And I didn't. So I left.

I decided to take the lead here since, out of everyone in the group, I had the most social skills. And that wasn't saying a lot.

"Excuse me!" I called, putting a little jog in my step as I hurried up the driveway.

Emily paused, and tension overtook her petite features. I'd done exactly what I didn't want to do. I'd scared her. Or maybe it was the fact there were three of us. Who wouldn't be intimidated by that?

"I'm not looking to buy anything." She pulled her bag up higher, like she wanted to use it as a shield . . . or maybe even a weapon.

"Oh, we're not salesmen," I said.

"I don't want you to paint my house either."

I paused, not following her logic. "You think we look like painters?"

What about my jeans and T-shirt screamed "painter"? Had the lack of paint stains on my shirt given me away?

She shrugged. "I know there's a group of college students going around the neighborhood, looking for work. Sorry."

Well, at least she thought we looked like college students. I liked the sound of that.

"Actually, we're PIs," I said, getting right to the point.

Emily's eyes widened. "PIs? Why are you here?"

"We have some questions for you," I said.

Sir Watson barked frantically in the background. The dog obviously had some anxiety issues and hated being left alone. Would he do to my car seats what he'd done to my couch? Bringing him had been a bad idea. Yet so had leaving him. As had letting him into my house and life.

It was a no-win situation.

Emily started at a quick pace toward her front door. "I don't have anything to say."

"Are you having an affair with Conrad?" Evie blurted, always the blunt one.

That stopped Emily, and something close to panic washed over her features. "Why would you ask that?"

Sherman shoved his glasses up higher and sounded

almost apologetic as he said, "Because I uncovered some hidden emails on his computer."

Emily drew in an almost imperceptible breath of air. "That program is supposed to erase them! They're supposed to be gone forever within five minutes of being sent. That's what the site said."

"Nothing is ever erased on the Internet." Sherman shrugged.

Emily's chin dropped toward her chest as she processed that—or as she formulated excuses. I wasn't sure which yet.

Finally, she raised her head, her gaze weary and resigned. "It's not what you think."

"What do we think?" Evie's voice held an edge of judgment.

"Conrad and I just started talking a couple months ago —after Brooke was already gone." She set her tote on the ground, the winter day bearable enough to have this conversation outside. "Conrad had nothing to do with her disappearance."

"How do you know that?" I asked. It was obvious Emily had already thought this through.

"Because he would never do something like that."

"If he's talking to you now, what makes you think there weren't others before you?" Evie asked, her words sharp.

"Because he's not that kind of guy." Emily's cheeks reddened, and she shoved a lock of hair behind her ear.

"Look, we just want to ask a few questions," Evie said.

Emily crossed her arms, almost as a comforting, protective gesture. "What do you want to know?"

I decided to step in before Evie decimated their conversation completely. "How'd you meet Conrad?"

"We were high school sweethearts, but we broke up after graduation. Conrad called me a year later and wanted to get back together, but it was too late. I was engaged to Arnie. Conrad said breaking up with me was the worst choice ever, and he begged me to reconsider. I didn't. Eventually he met Brooke, and I thought that was the end of it."

"And then?" Evie said.

"And then I heard that Brooke had disappeared, so I called Conrad to express my condolences. One thing led to another, and we decided to meet face-to-face to catch up. I thought it might be good for him to have someone to talk to."

"Yet you had to use a program that hid your messages," Evie said.

Emily narrowed her eyes. "We did. But it was only because Conrad said he was the police's prime suspect. He didn't want to add any fuel to the fire, and he knew this could make him look guilty."

"What happened after you met?" I asked.

"Seeing him again was wonderful." A sad smile crossed Emily's lips. "It made me realize how good we had been together. And Conrad felt the same way. We talked a lot about the past. The good old days, so to speak."

"Was that when he told you that you were the best kisser ever?" Evie asked.

Emily's cheeks turned red again. "He did. But that's as far as it went."

"What do you mean?" Evie asked, her invisible, truth-detecting antennae seeming to go on full alert.

Emily frowned. "I mean, I was interested in more. Seeing him made me wish I had broken things off with Arnie and gone back with Conrad instead all those years ago. And I think Conrad was tempted. But he said he still had hope that Brooke would return."

"Is that right?" Evie narrowed her eyes.

"It is. He decided it was best if we didn't speak anymore because it was too tempting. He didn't know when the right time to move on would be—or if there would be one. I took the breakup—if that's what you would even call it—hard. It's been lonely since my divorce." Her voice cracked.

I didn't know about Sherman and Evie, but I believed her. Conrad had gone to the line, but he hadn't necessarily crossed it and entered into Cheaterville. Or maybe he had. Emotionally, at least. I wasn't an expert on these things.

When was the right time in a situation like this? Had Brooke left him? Was she dead? And how long did a person hang on to hope?

"Is there anything that Conrad told you that made you

form any theories about his wife's disappearance?" I asked. It was a last-ditch effort, but sometimes the best ideas came from that last question, the last "Is there anything you want to add?"

Emily shook her head. "No, there's nothing."

Well, it was worth a try, at least.

"Except that he thinks something bad happened to her." Emily looked up nervously. "He doesn't think she would have left without saying anything. Said she was the kind who'd tell him and who'd be direct about something like that."

"She wasn't direct about her debt or her part time job," I pointed out.

Emily shrugged. "I'm just telling you what he said. I didn't know the woman. But if Conrad fell in love with her, she was—is—probably remarkable."

"I see," I said. "Thank you."

I turned to take a step away.

"There is one more thing," Emily said.

My heart skipped a beat as I turned back around. One more thing was usually a good sign. "What's that?"

"Conrad's neighbor should be a suspect," Emily said.

"The old man?" I remembered talking to him in the backyard. He'd seemed nice enough.

"I guess he has a criminal record. Conrad told me. He has blinders on toward the man and thinks of him like a grandfather. But he's not seeing clearly. I told him that."

No, that couldn't possibly be correct. Detective Belfield

would have mentioned it, right? "Why does this man have a criminal record?"

"Voyeurism."

My breath caught. The man had said he'd seen someone going through Conrad and Brooke's mailbox. Had he seen that because he'd been watching Brooke? Just how far did his curiosity with the woman go?

Now it was time to confer with the rest of the crew and figure out our next step.

fter getting stuck in traffic, Evie, Sherman, and I didn't get back to Norfolk until six that evening.

I needed to talk to either Conrad or his neighbor—possibly even both. My questions couldn't wait. Meanwhile, Sherman and Evie were going to do some research on Brooke's ex, Jason Kline. He lived in Colorado, so we wouldn't be able to pay him a visit. But Evie and Sherman could find out everything possible about him online and/or give him a call. They'd also been tasked with contacting Maranatha Health to confirm Brooke's part-time job.

I figured there was no harm in splitting up and then sharing what we'd learned. The control freak in me wanted to do it all on my own. But I knew this was a more effective use of our time and resources.

Besides, Sir Watson needed to get out of my car, even

though he seemed quite happy sitting beside me right now.

I pulled to a stop in front of Conrad's house—again. I'd contemplated whom to talk to first and decided on Conrad. I wanted to find out his take on the neighbor before investigating him myself.

Sir Watson walked beside me as I strode up to Conrad's door then rang the bell. Since it was already dark outside, I actually found a strange comfort in having my new hairy friend with me. Safety in numbers, and all. And, yes, dogs counted as a number.

Conrad answered five seconds later and stared at me in surprise.

"I have a feeling this isn't good," he started, leaning on the doorway as if bracing himself. He glanced at Sir Watson and seemed to tense even more.

"Why didn't you tell me about your neighbor?" I started.

Conrad blinked, either in surprise or to scoff my question. "Mr. Abe? What's there to tell?"

"Brooke was worried that he was a peeping tom."

Conrad shook his head, coming out of his shock. "The man is like a grandfather. He's a little quirky, but there's no crime in that."

"Is it correct he's been in jail?"

"He explained it to me. It was all a misunderstanding. He likes to watch the birds. He has a whole collection of birdhouses and other things in his backyard. Look and you'll see for yourself."

"So he was falsely accused of watching people when he was really watching birds?" I clarified. It definitely sounded like Conrad had some blinders on here.

"That's correct."

"Did he happen to be watching the birds whenever Brooke was outside?"

"What? No. Why would you think that?"

And here's where I went in for the sucker punch. "Emily Hayman told me."

The color drained from Conrad's face, and he backed up ever so slightly. "Emily and I are just friends."

"Then why didn't you tell me about her?" Seriously, could this guy dig himself any deeper? The truth was a much safer bet than keeping secrets.

Conrad ran a hand over his face, and his voice strained as he said, "Because I knew how it would look."

I crossed my arms, his oversimplified explanations annoying me. Actually, this whole investigation was starting to annoy me. Images of a real life "Gone Girl" haunted my thoughts. There had been too many lies. Too many secrets. Too much drama.

"When you hide stuff, it makes you look guilty." My voice sounded dull as I said the words.

"I'm sorry. But I promise there was nothing there."

I glanced at Mr. Abe's house, trying to form my next

plan of attack. It was obvious Conrad wasn't going to share anything else.

"Maybe I should talk to your neighbor. It seems like he's been keeping an eye on you. Maybe he's seen something."

"He hasn't seen anything because there hasn't been anything. Besides, he has some dementia and is in failing health. Don't bother the man. Please. He's been good to me, and he was good to Brooke."

Yet Mr. Abe had been spraying weeds. In March. I still wasn't sure that was normal. No, more likely he was keeping an eye on this house.

I needed to keep that in mind.

I went home and found Riley standing in the middle of the living room, looking equally as flabbergasted as I'd been. I hadn't had the chance to warn Riley about the disaster that was waiting for him at home.

"I guess it's a good thing we got that couch from someone who'd used it for twenty years first," Riley said, staring over the battleground.

"I guess it is."

His gaze went to Sir Watson. "Someone was up to some trouble today."

"That would be an understatement. And I already talked to Sierra. No one has called to claim him."

"Should we look for a rescue group?" Riley's frown deepened.

"It's not a bad idea." Though part of me felt horrible for saying it out loud. I knew rescue groups were good and helpful and the people who worked them were usually kind. But sending Sir Watson there felt a bit like sending a child away to foster care.

Which was ridiculous. This was a dog. And it had been a temporary arrangement from the start. There was nothing to feel guilty about.

Sir Watson whined beside me, almost as if he could understand. My heart pounded with a mix of regret and compassion.

Why did this dog have to like me so much? The canine wasn't going to make this easy, was he?

On that note, maybe I shouldn't have named him. Or bought him things. Or ever even let him into my house.

Because now I felt strangely connected—and ultimately responsible—for the beast.

"So, I want to hear about your day," Riley said, pacing toward the kitchen.

I released my breath. "I'd love to tell you about it. Let's pull out that leftover Chinese food."

Yep, I was that kind of spouse. The kind that ordered out and always got extra for leftovers.

And there was no shame in that.

CHAPTER TEN

*E*vie, Sherman, and I met to share what we'd learned over breakfast at The Grounds the next morning. The coffee shop was halfway between their hotel and my place—plus it had great coffee, which, yes, I had mentioned before.

We had only about thirty minutes to debrief before heading over to talk to Brooke's parents. Evie had called them last night to arrange the meeting. Maybe they would have some insight.

In the meantime, I'd left Sir Watson with Riley, who was able to work from home today. At least I wouldn't have to worry about the canine getting into trouble —for now.

With the comforting scent of my favorite things floating around us and more Ed Sheeran playing over-head, we all gave each other our updates.

Apparently, Sherman had called Maranatha Health either last night or this morning. He'd been able to talk to Brooke's manager there. According to her boss, Brooke was a great employee, always on time, and always polite. Nothing had happened on the job site that raised any red flags. In fact, her patients loved her. And she hadn't given notice before she disappeared.

Also, Sherman and Evie had confirmed that Brooke's ex-boyfriend, Jason Kline, was accounted for during the time of her disappearance. The government contract worker was negotiating a deal in the Middle East and had a rock solid alibi.

Even though I'd talked to Conrad last night and he'd pleaded his innocence, a better picture of the man was forming in my mind, and I'd come to one basic conclusion. Conrad was flighty.

Engineering had been his first job, but I had a feeling that teaching wouldn't be his last. Riley had also told me that Conrad had been into cross-country biking before participating in these obstacle-course competitions, and that the man had also mentioned that he liked to do magic shows when he was younger. That wasn't to mention the photography class Conrad had been taking when Brooke disappeared.

I had a feeling Conrad's love life was no different. Had he been unsure what he wanted in a woman and future spouse? Had he moved from relationship to relationship? My guess? Yes. Absolutely yes.

All of that, and I still didn't think the man was guilty in this.

Nor did I really think that Mr. Abe was guilty—even though I did want to keep him in mind.

Which led me to this meeting.

I took a sip of my drink—a vanilla latte, of course—and broke off a piece of my cinnamon scone as I looked at my notes.

"So this is what we know so far," I started. "It looks like we can rule out Conrad, Emily, and Jason—Brooke's ex. Also, this doesn't seem to be tied to Brooke's secret part-time job at Maranatha."

"That sounds right," Sherman said.

"There is still a possibility that this mystery man with the scarred face who showed up at the hospital could be involved," I said. "He possibly went through her mail at home as well."

"Sounds like a stalker." Sherman said it casually, like this was an ordinary conversation.

"Stalker or not, the likelihood of us finding him isn't good." Evie popped a grape into her mouth. "Which is too bad. Maybe he saw something."

"Or maybe he's responsible for all of this." Sherman shrugged and leaned back.

"If this was a random crime—a matter of being in the wrong place at the wrong time—then the likelihood of finding answers in general is nearly zero," I said. "Maybe that was why the case had gone cold."

"But we were hired to solve this," Sherman reminded us. "We've got to exhaust every lead."

"My thoughts exactly," I agreed. "And we should start with Brooke's parents."

After everything I'd heard about Brooke, I expected her parents to live in a fancy house in a nice part of town. Instead, they lived in an average house in an average part of town. And though the house and neighborhood might be average, their home was immaculately kept—on the outside, at least. I'd never seen flowerbeds look this good in the winter or grass so green I almost wondered if it had been dyed.

I got out of my car and stepped onto the sidewalk to examine the blades a moment when Evie and Sherman pulled up behind me. For some reason, Evie insisted on driving separately. I didn't really understand it, but, then again, I didn't understand Evie. It wasn't a battle I was going to fight right now.

They joined me, and we crossed the sidewalk to the glossy black door with a brass kickplate and knocker on the front. A few minutes later, an anxious-looking couple answered the door.

The woman looked like an older version of Brooke, and her eyes were red-rimmed, as if she'd been crying.

The man looked regal in his expensive sweater, but his expression was also solemn and sad.

This wasn't going to be a fun conversation. But it was necessary.

I decided to take the lead here. "I'm Gabby, and these are my friends Evie and Sherman. Thanks for agreeing to meet with us."

They introduced themselves but didn't offer any first names to make the conversation more casual or relaxed. Nope, it would be Mr. and Mrs. Winkle. They ushered us inside, to a nicely decorated house, and we sat on a navy-blue couch with glasses of cool water in our hands.

"Conrad hired you." Mrs. Winkle frowned as the words left her mouth.

"That's correct." I took a sip of my drink, already feeling the tension forming between my shoulders.

"I'm surprised he has money for that," Brooke's dad said, also with a frown and a distinctly bitter sound to his voice.

So some of this tension was over finances. Noted.

"Someone not connected to Conrad is funding the investigation," I said.

"I guess I'm glad to hear Conrad couldn't scrounge up money for this considering he made our daughter go to work." Mr. Winkle leaned back in his leather recliner, and a deep furrow formed on his brow.

Okay, there was definitely some resentment here.

Had the couple always been like this? Or had Brooke's disappearance saturated this house with sorrow?

"It sounds like you didn't have a great relationship with your daughter's husband." I kept my voice even in hopes of not escalating the tension in the air.

"Conrad is a nice enough guy, I suppose," Mr. Winkle said, absently rubbing the arm of the recliner with his thumb. "I just don't think he was always looking out for the best interests of our daughter. When Brooke got married, Conrad promised to be her provider. Just like I provided for my wife and family. But instead he broke that promise and forced her to finish her degree and get a job."

This all seemed a bit overstated. I mean, there were different strokes for different folks. Some couples liked traditional roles; others took a more modern approach. I wasn't sure that one was right and the other wrong. It was all a matter of the choices the couple made together.

Evie set her glass down on a coaster on the table beside her and crossed her ankles. "What do you think happened, Mr. and Mrs. Winkle?"

"I know one thing." Mrs. Winkle's voice cracked, her stoic expression along with it. "My daughter would never walk away from all of this without a word to us. No, we were close. She wouldn't do this to us."

I hated to bring this up but . . . "Did she tell you about her secret part-time job?"

Mr. Winkle's face clouded, as if he'd just drunk

lemonade spiked with vinegar. "No, she didn't. She must have been so miserable if she went as far as to do that. She probably knew we'd give Conrad a bad time about making our little girl work so hard while he was out following his dreams and his silly little hobbies."

What he said made sense, I had to admit. Maybe Conrad was a little selfish. Maybe both he and Brooke were. I wasn't sure, but the couple definitely hadn't learned the art of compromise.

"But you're confident she would have told you before leaving?" Evie clarified.

"That's right. Brooke would never put us through this worry if she had a choice," Mrs. Winkle said. "She was a kind, loving girl. That's why I thought, if she had to work, that nursing would be perfect for her. She truly loved people."

That was the second time I'd heard that. Slowly, my opinion about Brooke was morphing from a spoiled rich girl to a nice woman who liked nice things but had a good heart.

I took another sip of water. "So you think foul play was involved?"

"We do." Mrs. Winkle's voice cracked. "We have no idea what happened. But we do know that Conrad threatened to divorce Brooke when he found out how many things she'd charged."

Things she'd charged might be putting it lightly. I mean,

Brooke had rung up twenty thousand in debt. But I let them continue.

"And I also know Brooke was almost willing to go along with the divorce," Mr. Winkle said. "Especially after she found out about Emily."

CHAPTER ELEVEN

"Emily?" I croaked out.

Emily and Conrad hadn't started speaking until after Brooke disappeared. At least, that's what they'd both told me. Had the wool been pulled over my eyes? Had I believed them too easily? Then again, I had no evidence to the contrary. Still, I wanted to kick myself.

Evie, Sherman, and I all exchanged looks, and I knew exactly what they were thinking—the same thing I was thinking. We'd been duped.

"That's right," Mrs. Winkle said. "Why do you look surprised?"

"I thought they didn't get in touch again until after Brooke disappeared," I said.

"Well, that would be inaccurate," Mrs. Winkle said. "They reconnected a couple months before her disappearance. Brooke couldn't prove anything happened between them, but she was suspicious."

"And you're saying Conrad threatened a divorce?" Evie said. "How did Brooke respond to all of this?"

Conrad had mentioned something about that. But he hadn't mentioned it was because of Emily.

"She was devastated, of course," Brooke's mom said. "As far as Brooke was concerned, the writing was on the wall. Their marriage was over."

"Conrad didn't hint at any of this," I said. "He indicated they were trying to work through their problems."

"Then he was living in a dream world." Mr. Winkle's eyes narrowed. He looked off in the distance as if imagining himself throttling his daughter's husband. "The fact they couldn't have a baby was just the final straw that indicated they weren't meant to be together."

Wow. That sounded so harsh. And sad. And so many other things that I was still processing.

And why couldn't Conrad just give me the facts straight? Why did I have to keep going back to him for more information? It definitely made him seem like he was hiding something.

People hid things because they were guilty. So maybe everyone's first theory was right—the husband did do it.

And I didn't like that.

When I stepped out of the Winkles' house ten minutes later, my phone buzzed. I looked at my screen and saw it was one of Brooke's friends from work, Trina. I'd called her at the beginning of this case and asked her to be in touch if she remembered anything.

She'd sent a text.

I quickly read the words.

The police are here. I think it involves Brooke. Can you come now?

"I need to go to the hospital." I hurried toward my car, anxious to find out what was going on. "One of Brooke's friends said something is up. She thinks it involved Brooke. I've been wanting to go to the hospital anyway and see if any of the nurses who worked with Brooke had any ideas."

"You know no one there will talk to you," Evie quipped, following behind me. "HIPPA and all."

"Well, Trina will talk to me, and maybe that's enough." I didn't mean to sound short with Evie. I really didn't. But . . .

"It sounds like we should be talking to Conrad." Evie crossed her arms. "Just like I said all along."

"I am surprised by what Brooke's parents said. He didn't mention that he'd been talking to Emily for longer. Or that Brooke might want a divorce as well."

"I want to tail Conrad," Evie announced.

"Why would you do that?" I paused by the driver's side door and stared at Evie, wondering exactly what she was thinking.

She shrugged nonchalantly. "Because I'm still not

convinced he's not guilty, and I'd like to rule out that possibility."

"I see." I nodded slowly, thoughtfully. I supposed it couldn't hurt anything. "If that would make you feel better, why don't you and Sherman do that?"

Evie's eyes narrowed, as if that suggestion was not part of her plan. "Do you think two of us are really needed to tail someone?"

Poor Sherman. Her words almost sounded like a rejection. "You never know when things are going to turn dangerous."

"I suppose." Evie turned toward Sherman with a sigh. "We should get going then."

"You do realize Conrad is probably at school today?" I reminded her, leaning into my car. "And he probably can't leave until after the students leave?"

"Or is that what he thinks everyone else will think?" Evie paused dramatically—yet she was dead serious. "Who knows—maybe he sneaks away and does his dirty deeds during his lunchbreak. There's no time like the present to find out."

Evie always said everything with such confidence that it was hard to argue. I mean, it usually never stopped me. But she did make me think twice at times.

With that final conversation, we all went our separate ways.

Our deadline was ticking closer, and I really hoped today proved to be productive.

As I wandered to the third floor of the hospital, I glanced around. I hated the smell and feel of this place. I knew hospitals could do great things—that the staff could heal people. Doctors had helped me out plenty of times when I'd gotten into scrapes.

But the bad memories also overwhelmed me. Memories of Riley being here. Of being unsure if he would survive. Of seeing all my plans for the future melt like a candle in the scorching sun.

I pushed away the memories and followed the signs until I reached the labor and delivery area. Just as I spotted the front desk, a woman was rushed past me in a wheelchair, holding her stomach and screaming in agony. Her husband or boyfriend—I assumed—followed her, holding up his phone, most likely in camera mode.

I cringed when I thought about the pain that woman was about to go through. Deep inside, I knew childbirth was beautiful. But my surface reaction? Man, was that going to be painful.

Nope, I wasn't in any hurry to have kids. I couldn't even handle a dog, apparently.

Once I got closer, I spotted Macy behind the desk area. Her eyes widened when she saw me, and she motioned me over.

"Gabby. What are you doing here?" She glanced around, as if she feared getting in trouble.

"I got a lead," I whispered.

Before she could ask any more questions, a tall, Eastern European-looking woman wearing scrubs joined us, a standoffish look in her eyes. "You must be Gabby."

"I am. Trina?"

"That's me." Some of her standoffish look disappeared. "Thanks for coming. We need to talk somewhere private."

She nodded toward the hall, indicating I should follow her. We walked toward the end of the corridor, away from most of the patients, and toward an area where the offices were located. Trina didn't seem like the small-talk type, nor did we have a lot of time, so I jumped into my questions.

"What's going on?" I asked.

"I heard something today that I need to share with someone. One of the hospital doctors here was accused of prescription drug fraud," she whispered. "Apparently, he created false patient files and prescribed pain killers to these 'fake people.' The DEA caught him and came in today to question him. They talked to several of us nurses as well to see if we knew anything then they left with both the doctor and his computer."

"That's interesting, but what's it have to do with Brooke?"

"I was standing near the door when the DEA talked to him," she said. "I overheard some things. It sounds like Brooke helped him."

My adrenaline seemed to flatline into dull, stunned silence. "What?"

Her face twisted, like her loyalty was at odds with reality. I'd been there before.

"I don't want to believe it either," Trina whispered. "Maybe Brooke was being set up. But the truth is that the police checked the computer records. Brooke was the one logged in when these records were created."

That didn't sound good. Maybe Brooke really did have a side business going on.

"Now the police are going to think Brooke felt guilty about what she was doing and took off," Trina continued.

I studied Trina's worried expression, trying to get a read on her thoughts. "Do you think Brooke would do that?"

"No. Absolutely not. But it doesn't look good." Trina's movements were tense and uncertain.

And, no, it really didn't look good for Brooke Murphy right now.

"One other thing," Trina muttered, looking back and forth down the hallway. "I talked to Brooke on the day she disappeared. She seemed happy."

That revelation really didn't seem all that revealing, but I'd see where she went with this. "Did she say why?"

"She said she'd found the solution to her problems."

"And that solution was . . ."

Trina straightened as another nurse walked by. She offered a friendly nod. As soon as the other woman passed, she bent toward me again and lowered her voice. "Brooke didn't say. I asked, and she said she had to confirm some things first. I didn't really give much thought to it. Until today."

"She gave no indication as to what that solution might be?"

"None whatsoever. But there were three things she wanted. She wanted her husband to stop getting mad at her, she wanted to pay off her debt, and she wanted a baby. So I assume it had something to do with one, if not all three, of those things."

"I see." Had doing favors for one of the local doctors been the solution to all her problems? I didn't want to believe it. But it was a possibility.

"I also heard the DEA mention something about Goodwin Pharmacy," Trina rushed on. "I think that's where some of these scripts were being filled."

"That's good to know. Thank you."

Trina's pager buzzed. "I've got to get to a patient. I just wanted to let you know, though."

I watched Trina walk away and remained where I was, watching people around me and absorbing her words.

As I heard screams coming from another room, I listened to the agony of childbirth for a moment. Sure, it was beautiful. Sure, babies were cute. But all of this was too much for this newlywed.

I started to walk away when Macy called me over.

"Did you get a lead?" she asked.

I shrugged, not wanting to give away too much information, especially if it would put Trina's job in jeopardy. "Maybe."

"I saw those men from the DEA come in earlier. Did it have something to do with them?"

"That's what I'm trying to figure out."

Macy frowned. "I hope you find answers. Because I know that with every day that goes by, the chances of Brooke coming home become less likely. The world would lose a good woman if that happened."

Was Brooke a good woman? Was she a good woman who'd gotten trapped in a bad situation? Or was there a dark side to Brooke that no one knew about?

CHAPTER TWELVE

*E*vie and Sherman were still following Conrad, who, based on our brief conversation, hadn't left school all day. I bit my tongue and didn't tell them it was a waste of time. I'd let them discover it for themselves. As long as I wasn't there waiting, I was fine with it.

Mostly.

And since they were occupied, I decided to pay a visit to the pharmacy. I knew privacy laws would be in effect, so I didn't know how much I'd be able to find out. It was worth a shot, though.

The place was near the oceanfront in Virginia Beach, but it wasn't part of a chain. No, it was a small, privately owned business that still sold ice cream, root beer floats, and grilled cheese sandwiches in the back corner.

Adorable.

I went straight to the Band-Aid aisle and pretended to be looking at a multipack. But I was really watching the people behind the counter—one pharmacist and two techs.

The pharmacist was an older man with white hair but remarkably smooth skin. He remained busy in the back. Two ladies worked at the front. One was an older black woman who didn't offer any smiles or warm interactions with any of the three customers at the counter. The other was a younger woman with blonde hair that was pulled into a sloppy ponytail. Her eyes darted about, and the quickness of her laugh and smile indicated possible insecurity.

I nibbled on my lip a moment, trying to figure out my plan of action.

I had to face the fact that I didn't have a plan.

Which stunk.

What kind of PI was I?

I couldn't just stand here all day, though.

I could think of absolutely no questions to ask about bandages, so instead I turned around and grabbed two different kinds of vitamins. I moseyed up to the counter and waited for the young blonde to see me.

She greeted me with an overly friendly smile. "Can I help you?"

I glanced at her name tag. Buttercup? Was that really her name? Like the heroine from *The Princess Bride*?

It didn't matter right now. I cleared my throat and smiled. "What's the difference between this magnesium oxide and magnesium citrate?"

"I don't know, but I can find out." She took the bottles from me, went back to talk to the pharmacist, and came back to me a few seconds later. "Okay, so this magnesium oxide is a less complete form, whereas magnesium citrate has a more solid bioavailability. In other words, it's better absorbed."

That meant nothing to me. "That's so helpful. Thank you."

She leaned closer. "Are you having bathroom issues?"

I flinched. "Excuse me?"

"Magnesium helps get you moving, if you know what I mean."

My cheeks heated. "Well, no. My doctor just mentioned it as a supplement I should add . . . to my rapidly growing stash. I'll take this one." I smiled and held up the citrate form.

She rang me up, apparently satisfied with my answer. "I heard it's beautiful outside," she said.

Good. She was a talker.

Talkers were good when it came to finding out information.

"Oh, it's so nice," I said. "Maybe you can enjoy it a little bit on your break."

"I wish I had time, but I'm going to grab something in

our little snack area in the back. It's what I do every day."
She frowned and pointed to the keypad in front of me.

I swiped my debit card. "Do they have anything good? I was thinking about giving it a try myself."

"Oh, I love their burgers. I know it's a pharmacy, so they're not supposed to have great food, but I really like it."

I punched in my information, my part of the transaction complete. "Good to know."

She glanced at her watch. "Speaking of which, after I ring you up, I'm on break."

"I might see you over there then." I paid, took my bag, and started toward that area.

There were three booths set up, and one was taken by a mom with two kids. I ordered my burger and fries and a soda. After I filled my own cup from the fountain, I wandered toward the booths.

And just in time.

Perky Buttercup was headed this way.

I glanced around and saw a yellow caution cone near a freshly mopped floor. I grabbed it and put it near the other booth.

Then I slid into the only remaining seat and waited to see if this plan would work.

As Buttercup came over, her eyes glanced around before meeting mine.

"Fancy seeing you here," I muttered, hating myself just a little.

"What's wrong with that booth?"

"I think the tabletop is wobbly." I shrugged and hesitated. "You're welcome to sit with me. Some company would be nice."

"Are you sure you don't mind?"

"Not at all. My husband would rather me talk to you and get in some of my ten thousand words of conversation than go home and completely exhaust him after work with my chatter."

Buttercup laughed. "I think I'll have that exact same problem one day. Let me order, and I will sit with you. Thanks."

I tried not to look too pleased. But I was. I really, really was.

"So, how long have you worked here?" I started, picking up one of my fries and trying to sound casual.

"About a year. My mom doesn't like it. She wanted me to go to college. But I just couldn't see myself paying all that money without really knowing what I really wanted to do with my life."

"At least you're making some money while you figure it out, right?"

She nodded. "That's right. And everyone here is so nice."

"Is it a fun job?"

"I don't know if I'd say fun, but I do get to meet a lot of nice people."

"I'm sure not everyone is nice."

"Oh, they're not. We have irate customers. Sick customers. Customers agitated by the price of their prescriptions."

"That's not even to mention the opioid crisis and prescription drug fraud," I added, munching on one of my french fries.

"Yes, exactly. I try to stay upbeat, but there's some crazy stuff going on out there." She took a long sip of her soda, reminding me a bit of a little girl—all innocence and naivete.

I didn't want to exploit that. But I did want answers, which meant I was going to have to make some choices about how to proceed.

Very carefully, I decided. "What's your biggest headache?"

"Trying not to be nosy." She shrugged and leaned closer, still gripping her soda. "You see some people come in and get the same pain meds every week, and you have to wonder."

"I bet."

She waved her hand in the air. "Listen to me. I'm saying entirely too much."

"No, I think that's interesting. I mean, prescription drug fraud is huge right now."

"I know. In fact, just today we got a call from someone

with the DEA. They're tracking a doctor who fabricated patient files and wrote fake prescriptions."

"That sounds horrible. Yet so interesting." I didn't have to fake that interest. Nope, not at all.

"I know! Tell me about it." She finished off her sandwich and ran a napkin over her lips.

"So, how can you help?" I asked.

"Well, the DEA came in and talked to the pharmacist, who then talked to me and Sandra. If we see anyone come in whose script is from this doctor, I have to tell the pharmacist, who will then call this DEA agent. Then we have to stall the person picking up the medicine until the agent gets here. Cool, right?"

"Totally cool. Totally Hollywood, for that matter."

Her grin widened. "I know! Isn't it?"

I pushed the rest of my food aside, honestly no longer interested. Her story was much more fulfilling. "You're like a secret agent. I've always wanted to be a secret agent. Instead, I do workshops."

I was building rapport and trying to tread carefully here so I wouldn't scare Buttercup away.

"What kind of workshops?"

I shrugged, absently playing with a chip on the tabletop. "The boring kind. I teach people how to use products that my company creates."

I didn't mention they were crime-scene investigation products. That would make it sound too cool.

"Yeah, that sounds boring." She frowned dramatically and glanced at her watch.

Her break would most likely be coming to an end soon. I needed to hasten this conversation.

I leaned closer. "Hey, I know this sounds weird. Really weird, for that matter. But, if this all goes down, could you call me too? I'd love to see it. It would make my week. Month. Okay, actually my year. For real. I try to live vicariously through other people."

"I do the same thing!" Buttercup squealed. Then her excitement dimmed, and she seemed to get lost in her thoughts. "But I'm not sure that would be a good idea."

"What could it hurt? Did they tell you not to?"

"I guess not. But . . ."

I leaned back before I looked overly eager. "Don't do anything you're uncomfortable with," I added. "It was just an idea. A stupid one at that. I just find real-life *Law and Order* scenarios so interesting."

She released a long, slow breath before straightening with decision. "You know what? Sure. I can let you know when it goes down. I don't see where it would hurt—unless you know a person coming in with the script from this doctor or something. You don't know anyone coming in with a script do you?"

"That would be a crazy coincidence if I did. And I don't even know the doctor's name."

She let out a feeble laugh. "That's what I thought. I'll

let you know. Just don't tell anyone. I don't want to get in trouble."

"Oh, I don't want to get you in trouble either. This is totally between us."

Buttercup smiled. "Then it's a deal."

CHAPTER THIRTEEN

Evie, Sherman, and I met back with each other at five. Evie had insisted on meeting at a restaurant close to Conrad's. His neighborhood only had one entrance, so if he left again, we should be able to spot him. In theory, at least.

The place was a hole-in-the-wall sandwich shop, so I didn't complain. A buffalo chicken wrap sounded like just the thing to end this day. I couldn't wait to hear what Evie and Sherman found out and to share my update with them.

They were already chowing down when I showed up, involved in some kind of intense—and quiet—conversation. Cooks worked behind a grill, the metal of their spatulas hitting the metal of the cooktop surface. Sizzles filled the air, along with the scent of onions and peppers.

If I remembered correctly, this place was known for

their cheesesteaks. Despite that, I still ordered my buffalo chicken wrap at the counter, and the employee promised to deliver it shortly.

"Hey guys." I dropped my purse beside them and stared at them, waiting to be let in on whatever it was they were speaking about so quietly.

To my surprise, Evie offered a tight smile instead. "Hi, Gabby."

It was like she was trying too hard to be polite, which made warning flags rise in my mind.

"What's going on?" I asked.

"Oh, nothing." Evie took another bite of her sandwich—it looked like egg salad on rye. Or did she strategically keep her mouth occupied so she wouldn't have to say anything else?

I knew because I'd used that technique before.

"Any Conrad updates?" There was something here. I was sure of it. My Sherlock senses were firing at full force.

"Nope," Evie said. "He went to school. Stopped by the grocery store afterward. And now he's home."

"So what's the secret?" I glanced back and forth from Sherman to Evie as they glanced back and forth at each other, unspoken conversation flowing as abundantly as honey in the Promised Land.

"We actually talked to one of the teachers going into the building," Evie started. "She said they're not allowed to leave for lunch—the only way they can leave the building is if they're taking personal time."

"Yeah, I kind of figured that." A woman at my church taught in the neighboring town of Chesapeake, and she liked to talk about work every chance she got.

"That's when we realized that sitting outside the school all day would probably be a colossal waste of time," Evie said.

I was certain she was going somewhere with this. I just didn't know where. "But you did it anyway? Or you figured out something else to do?"

They exchanged another look, and my agitation grew.

"We found something else to do," Evie finally said, holding her sandwich but not bothering to eat it.

I waited, letting the awkward silence speak for itself.

"We went to Newport News," Evie blurted.

Newport News was across the river. The town was nowhere on my radar with this investigation. "That's forty-five minutes away. Why would you do that?"

Evie put down her sandwich and frowned. "I actually went to check out something concerning my mother's disappearance."

"In Newport News?" Something wasn't clicking in my mind. "I thought you were from Texas."

"I am. But I told you the last time my mom was seen was after she met a man online."

"Right . . ." We'd had a heart–to–heart during our last investigation, and Evie had told me about how her foster mom had gone on a date with a man she met online and she'd never been seen again.

I thought that talk had broken down walls, but I was no longer certain of that.

"I had Sherman track down this guy's online presence. His name is Ed Wilson. It turns out he dated someone else he met online, and she lives in Newport News."

I popped a chip in my mouth and slowly chewed on it. "So you went to find the woman?"

"Exactly. And we did find her." Evie pressed her lips together, as if choosing her words carefully.

"What did she have to say?" Evie had my attention now.

"Her name is Linda, and she actually did go on a couple of dates with Ed Wilson. Said he was nice enough."

"Is there a *but* in there?"

"The only but is in the fact that this woman is still alive and well and said this guy showed no signs of being violent or weird."

"Which makes you think he didn't do anything to your mom?"

"She's the third woman I've talked to that he dated. Everyone seems to be okay."

"Did you talk to the guy himself?"

"He's actually been out of the country on business for the past few months."

"Did you confirm that?" I asked.

Evie nodded. "I did. He left thirteen weeks ago to

work on a project in Spain. He's a contractor for the military."

"Do you still think he's a suspect?"

She drew her lips together in a tight line. "No, I actually don't. I wonder if I've been off track this whole time."

"Well, at least you're able to mark that off and move on."

Evie nodded. "That's right. I'm sorry I didn't mention it earlier. I know we're being paid to investigate this case, but I just couldn't give up this opportunity."

"It's okay. I want you to figure out what happened with your mother. I know it's important to you."

"Thank you for understanding."

"Of course." I ate one last potato chip and leaned back. The conversation had taken an unexpected turn and had reminded me about life—and issues—outside the scope of this investigation. I could get a little too focused for my own good sometimes.

"How about you, Gabby?" Sherman asked, pushing away his empty basket. "Did you find out anything?"

I told them about what I'd learned, and they both perked up at the information.

"So you're thinking prescription drug fraud? Why didn't you say so sooner?" Evie said. "That could be quite lucrative."

I resisted giving her a dirty look. "I don't want to believe that Brooke would take things that far in her quest to get out of debt."

Evie gave me one of her know-it-all looks. "But just because you don't want to believe it doesn't mean she didn't take it this far."

I couldn't argue with that, even though part of me wanted to take the ketchup bottle on the table and squirt it in her face. I would never do that. Of course. But it was tempting. "You're right."

"You really think that pharm tech will call you back if someone brings in a script from this doctor?" Sherman asked.

I shrugged. "It's hard to say. But I don't know how else to track a possible connection between Brooke's disappearance and this prescription drug fraud."

"I may be able to help." Sherman sat up straighter, his eyes wavering with a touch of awkwardness.

I twisted my head so I could look at him straight on. "How would you do that?"

"There are back doors into records like that—records that are being kept online."

Everything else seemed to fade from my mind at that moment. The jazzy overhead music. The scent of fresh bread. Evie's persnickety gaze.

I licked my lips. "Isn't that illegal?"

"It is." Sherman pushed his glasses up higher on his nose. "If you're caught, you can get in trouble. That's why I never get caught."

"I don't want to pressure you into doing anything you're not comfortable with." I'd pushed the limits before, but this felt as if I was really pushing the limits.

Sherman shrugged. "No pressure."

Evie's eyes lit as she turned toward Sherman. "This is a side of you I've never seen before."

His shoulders seemed a little straighter and his chin higher. "I don't always play it safe."

Her eyebrows flickered up. "Interesting. I like that."

Great. Doing something illegal was what might bring them together.

I supposed it could be worse.

Or maybe not.

I left Evie and Sherman to do their illegal backdoor hacking thing at the hotel, and I went to Conrad's house to have yet another face-to-face with the man.

I had a few questions for him that I needed to address. Now.

His eyes widened when he opened his door and saw me standing there. "Gabby. Again."

I quickly noted his workout clothes. He planned on heading to the gym. "Sorry to stop by unexpectedly."

He extended his arm behind him. "Come in."

I had a few reservations about stepping inside. But I did it anyway. However, I didn't make any move to sit down or accept a drink. No, I just wanted to get right to the point. And I did have my gun in my purse, if worst came to worst. I'd almost lost my life enough times that I hardly ever left home without it.

"You haven't been straight with me." I crossed my arms, knowing my body language was uninviting—and wanting to use that to my advantage.

Conrad's cheeks turned pink. "What do you mean?"

I started to answer but paused. The living room beyond him caught my eye. Yesterday, it had been messy with a coffee mug left out and a strewn blanket. Now it was back to looking pristine.

"You cleaned," I murmured.

"Is that a crime?"

I turned back to him, my thoughts churning. "Why did you leave it messy for us?"

The pink on his cheeks turned to red. "I don't know what you're talking about."

I was growing weary of these games. Very, very weary. "It's like this. At the restaurant on the first day we met, you made every effort to ensure everything was in order and straight at our table. Yet when my friends and I got here to look at your house, it was messy, almost like you didn't have OCD tendencies. Now it's straight. Why?"

Conrad's muscles bristled from his biceps to his neck. "It's stupid, really."

I'd be the judge of that—and I was really good at judging stupid. "I'm listening."

He ran a hand over his face. "I figured if you came

over and I had everything spick-and-span clean that you might get suspicious and think I staged things to look innocent. So I made myself leave it unkempt. It went against every fiber of my being."

"You thought about it that much?" I was having trouble buying this.

"I did. I know how things look." He sighed and leaned against the wall near the front door, almost like the pressure was too much. "I didn't want to set myself up."

Once someone lied about something, I didn't put it past them to lie about anything. But his excuse might be believable. Then again, maybe I'd given this guy one too many chances.

I narrowed my eyes, not wanting to let on that I was giving him a break. "When did you really start talking to Emily? Brooke's parents seem to think it was before their daughter disappeared."

He let out a long breath. Took a step back. Rocked forward.

Obvious signs of distress.

And guilt.

Just what was the truth here?

CHAPTER FOURTEEN

"Emily and I did reconnect a couple months before Brooke disappeared. But nothing happened." The veins at Conrad's temples and neck bloated with emotion. "It was purely friendship with zero romantic undertones."

I tried not to sigh, but I did anyway. Games like this really annoyed me. Almost as much as the Broadway musical adaptation of Stephen King's novel *Carrie*. Who had ever thought that would be a good idea?

"Why did you keep that information from us?" I asked, feeling a bit like a broken record.

"Because I know how it looks."

"How did you get rid of that information online and keep it a secret? There should be some kind of electronic trail showing the two of you had been talking. The police would have discovered that."

"It's not like that. I actually ran into Emily at an area-wide teacher's conference," he said. "And that's where it ended. I told Brooke about seeing her, and she seemed a little jealous. But Emily and I didn't start talking again until after Brooke disappeared. That part of the story was true."

I might believe him—except he'd already kept so much from me. "If you continue to keep things from me, I'm dropping this case. I don't like being lied to. And I don't like it when people waste my time. Taking this case was a big mistake."

Conrad's face dipped. "I'm sorry. I really am. I just didn't want you to think I'm guilty—like everyone else does. I see the looks people give me. I hear them whispering behind my back. Half the time, I'm waiting for the police to show up and arrest me. But I didn't do this. I wouldn't have hurt my wife. Please believe me."

Why did he have to sound so convincing? My gut told me he hadn't hurt his wife. But, on occasion, my gut was wrong.

Still, I had to make a choice. Did I believe Conrad? Or did I walk away?

Some part of me told me not to give up. Not yet. I only hoped I didn't regret this.

I raised my chin. "Like I said—you have one more chance, and then I'm out."

"Thank you, Gabby. This means a lot to me."

I stepped outside a minute later. As I did, I saw a car

pull away from the front of the house.

I paused. Had the driver been keeping an eye on us? Was this what Conrad meant when he said someone was watching him?

I didn't know.

But there was something about this case that I really didn't like. I had a feeling the implications of whatever was going on here ran far deeper than I originally thought.

It seemed weird not to work until all hours of the night, but I had not only a new marriage but also a new house and a dog to divide my time with. I supposed there were disadvantages to doing cases in your own hometown. Namely, life. Not that life was a disadvantage. I was just used to working around the clock every case I got. But I needed to learn to balance that with time for family and friends.

Sherman had promised to continue looking into prescription drug fraud, as well as into tracking the orders at the pharmacy. Evie was going to continue to work on her psychological profile.

Before I could think about it for too long, I opened the front door to my house. Just as the scent of garlic, basil, and tomatoes hit my nostrils, I heard a loud sound. A *stampeding* sound.

Sir Watson. And he was headed toward me.

I braced myself for impact.

And I got it.

His paws hit my shoulders and threw me back into the wall. Then a wet tongue covered my face. Over and over again.

I wanted to fuss. But instead, I giggled. What was wrong with me?

"Down, Sir Watson. What are you doing?" Laughter still clung to my voice, which made it sound way less authoritative.

Riley appeared around the corner, an oven mitt on his hand and an expression of surprise on his face. "Someone is happy to see you. And so is Watson."

"You are so sweet." I leaned toward Riley and kissed his cheek. It just didn't seem right to hit his lips with mine when Sir Watson had just been licking my face. "What are you cooking?"

"Lasagna."

I frowned and remembered my buffalo chicken wrap. "Man. I wish I knew. I just met the gang for an update."

"I figured as much. We can always have it for leftovers all week."

I was so blessed to have a man like Riley in my life. "Look at you, cooking and everything."

"Well, it's actually lasagna made with eggplant. I'm trying to be healthier."

My excitement level went down a few notches. But

Riley was still sweet. "Gearing up for your competition?"

"Trying to."

Lucky chirped in the background, reminding me how much easier it was to take care of a parrot as opposed to . . . oh, I don't know. Let's say a dog.

Despite that, I rubbed Sir Watson's head. "How did he do today?"

"Great. No problems at all."

Of course, he'd been on his best behavior around Riley. "No word on who he belongs to yet?"

"No. I ran into Sierra, and she hadn't heard anything. We'll need to figure out how long we're going to keep him because at this rate, it could be long-term."

I glanced at Sir Watson, who now sat beside me, wagging his tail. His bright eyes followed my every move.

It was like the dog knew what we were talking about and wanted to be on his best behavior.

Actually, it was kind of sweet. But the words "long-term" made my stomach tighten.

"We do have a dilemma, don't we? And we need to get a new couch." I scowled as I looked over at the remains of our mutilated couch cushions.

Just then, my phone buzzed. It was a text from Macy.

The scuttlebutt at work is that Brooke was helping Dr. Heath set up fake patient files. Is it true? Because I did see her talking to the good doctor on multiple occasions.

CHAPTER FIFTEEN

On my way out to meet Evie and Sherman the next morning, I ran into Chad. He was dressed in his construction gear—old jeans and a ratty T-shirt—when we met in the driveway. I, on the other hand, was dressed in another one of my favorite T-shirts, this one reading "No Drama Llama," with a gray blazer, jeans, and some respectable flats. It was forty degrees and just a little too chilly for my signature flip-flops.

"You still have the dog, I see," Chad said as he loaded a toolbox into the back of his truck.

"We still have the dog. No calls on him. It's hard to believe." Like, so hard that I nearly felt set up.

As if on cue, Sir Watson barked in the distance.

"Sir Watson doesn't want you to go." Chad nodded toward my place.

I looked back and saw the dog's face pressed against

the glass of my front window. Had he somehow learned how to get out of his kennel? That dog . . .

"He's a smart one," Chad remarked.

Against all my wishes, my heart squeezed.

I never knew I was such a softie for animals until now.

And then I wondered what else the dog might destroy.

I frowned as I pictured coming home to a house with ruined wooden floors or chewed-up end tables.

"You know, I think maybe I'll take him with me," I muttered. "He's trouble."

Chad shrugged, his gaze still on my window. "Might be a good police dog."

"Sir Watson?" Certainly I hadn't heard correctly. I almost snorted. That dog was only good for making my life complicated.

"German shepherds are used in police work all the time," Chad continued.

I couldn't argue about German shepherds. But Sir Watson was not your average German shepherd. He was beyond hope. "He's too old to be trained."

"No, I just read an article about how rescue dogs are being trained. You can teach an old dog new tricks. Besides, isn't he only about a year old?"

I'd hoped he wouldn't remember that detail. "Maybe. But it doesn't matter. We probably won't be keeping him."

Sir Watson barked at the window again, as if telling me I was wrong. If dogs could laugh, that canine was probably holding his side and bellowing with amusement in his own little doggy way.

"But the question is: Will he be keeping you?" Chad gave me a pointed look.

I ignored him. I couldn't even go there mentally right now. "On another note, where are you headed this morning?"

Chad did a mix of construction jobs and crime-scene cleanup, depending on how open his schedule was. Or how desperate he was for work.

"I'm finishing a bathroom remodel," he said. "But I thought about you this morning when I was watching the news."

"Why's that?"

"You remember how you used to scour news stories and then go to the crime scene so you could drop off your card?"

I'd had to do whatever it took to get business. Could you fault a girl for that? "Yes, guilty as charged."

"Did you hear about that body found in the woods this morning?"

"No, I haven't had the news on. What are the details?" I couldn't resist asking. Crimes, you know. They were terrible and fascinating.

"I don't know much." Chad walked around to the other side of the truck, ready to leave. "The woman hasn't been identified yet. Not last I heard. All I know is that the body appeared to be a woman in her late twenties with blonde hair."

As he said the words, the blood drained from my face.

Brooke. Had the police found Brooke?

I had to get down to the police station.

~

I headed out to see Detective Belfield. But first I'd called my friend Clarice and convinced her to go to my house to dog-sit. There was no way I could bring Sir Watson with me for this. I told her where I hid my spare key—reminding myself to hide it somewhere different later—and I was on my merry way.

Then I called Evie and Sherman and updated them.

"Definitely check that out," Evie said. "We'll tail Conrad again."

"Sounds like a plan."

I hung up, and my mind raced. The area where that body had been found wasn't far from the resort area where Brooke's car had been left. How long had the body been there? How had the woman died? Did Conrad know about this yet?

The questions collided in my head.

I didn't have the answers. But I was determined to find them.

I stopped at the station, knowing there was a good chance that this wouldn't get me anywhere. And it didn't.

The receptionist told me Detective Belfield wasn't in.

And that was when I decided to head to the crime scene. I knew where it was, thanks to Chad. And I figured the police were probably still there.

I was treading turbulent waters right now—this could cause some bad blood between me and the police if I didn't play my cards right. So I needed to play them right.

I pulled up to a decent-sized state park on the edge of Virginia Beach, a park that had a beach, a maritime forest, plenty of swamps, and tons of hiking trails. It didn't take me long to find the huddle of police cruisers in a secluded parking lot at the other side of the property.

I parked not too far away and moseyed toward the swarm of cops. None of them paid me much attention.

So I listened for a moment.

And then they noticed me. One of the uniforms turned to address me. "Can I help you?"

"I'm looking for Detective Belfield."

"Are you a reporter?" he asked.

"I'm not."

"Well, the detective is busy right now. But I can let him know you stopped by."

"I really need to talk to him. I'm . . . I'm a PI."

The uniform looked unimpressed and maybe even more unwilling to help. "Sorry."

Was he apologizing that he couldn't assist me? Or was it because he felt sorry for me as a measly PI? It didn't matter.

My shoulders slumped. I couldn't just leave here with nothing. But—

Just then, Belfield stepped from the woods. As soon as he saw me, recognition flashed in his eyes. "Mrs. Thomas."

"Can I have a moment of your time?" I asked, quickly following on his heels as he strode to his car.

"I'm sorry. We're in the middle of an active investigation. I can't speak about what's going on. I'm assuming that's what you're going to ask."

"Can you just tell me if it's Brooke Murphy you found?"

He offered a terse shake of his head. "I can't answer that question."

"I heard the body matches Brooke's description."

"It doesn't matter. I can't give you any details. I'm sorry. I know you want to solve this. But you have to leave the police work to the actual police."

I took that as a challenge.

"What about the fake scripts being written at the hospital where Brooke worked?" I asked.

That stopped the detective cold in his tracks. He froze and stared at me a moment. "You know about that?"

I shrugged. "I am an investigator. A good one."

Finally, he nodded. "Well, color me impressed. And, I'm sorry, Mrs. Thomas, but I can't answer your questions. I would if I could, but I've got a family at home to feed. I can't afford to lose this job."

And even I couldn't argue with that one.

I called Evie and Sherman. They hadn't gotten anywhere in tailing Conrad. We were going to meet in the school parking lot, but just as I arrived there my phone rang.

It was Buttercup.

From the pharmacy.

I almost couldn't believe my own eyes when I saw her number.

I answered on Bluetooth and tried to keep my excitement at bay.

"This is Buttercup from Goodwin's Pharmacy," she rushed. "A guy is here with a prescription from the doctor who's being investigated. I know you said you wanted to see for yourself. Apparently, he's one of the fabricated identities that the DEA is monitoring."

"Did you call the DEA?" I found myself whispering also and shook my head to snap myself out of it.

"Yes, they're sending someone out. I'm not sure how this will all go down."

"Thanks for letting me know."

"His prescription will be ready in twenty so get here as soon as you can if you want to see it happen real time."

"Okay. Thanks again."

I hung up, and excitement surged through my blood. Maybe we were getting our first real lead.

Or, then again, maybe this had nothing to do with Brooke's disappearance. We could be following a great lead for a crime that had nothing to do with the one we were being paid to investigate.

I motioned for Evie and Sherman to join me in my car. As soon as they were in with doors closed and seatbelts on, I took off, filling them in as I drove.

"Maybe we've actually got a lead," Evie said. "Feels like a near miracle."

I wanted to argue with her. I really did. But I couldn't. Evidence was trickling in for this case more slowly than high school flunkies headed for their last day of class.

"I did some research into prescription drug fraud," Sherman started.

I wove between cars, trying to get to the pharmacy in time. "Let's hear it."

"Okay, there are a couple of ways people can be involved," Sherman said. "One of the most common ways is to pay off a doctor to write the scripts for you. It sounds like this is what happened at Brooke's hospital. I'm sure the doctor was well paid for his role."

"And now he'll probably lose his license and face jail time," Evie said.

"Exactly," Sherman said. "Other times, people will steal prescription pads and forge the information. But scripts are mostly done on computers now and sent electronically. Whenever a doctor prescribes a suspicious amount of pain-relief narcotics, it's flagged by the DEA."

"Okay," I said.

"If Brooke somehow got involved in this, it could have been lucrative," Sherman said. "She could have paid off her debt faster. Stopped working another job. It could have been the solution she was looking for."

I didn't want to believe it. I really didn't. But that was looking more and more likely. Maybe the good girl had been afraid of being discovered for her wrongdoing, and then she hit the road before she could get caught.

I pulled into the pharmacy. It was time to get this party started.

CHAPTER SIXTEEN

Evie and Sherman decided to stay in the car. All three of us being inside might look too suspicious. I didn't spot any law enforcement vehicles outside. However, the DEA probably drove unmarked sedans. Still, none of the vehicles looked professional—from an open-top Jeep to a few clunkers to a Mercedes SUV.

It had taken me almost exactly twenty minutes to get here, so I knew I was cutting this close. I tried to look casual as I entered the store and paused.

I scanned my surroundings, stopping in the pharmacy area to my left. A lone man sat in a chair there, reading a magazine and waiting. He had an olive complexion and wore a black suit. The man seemed unassuming enough, I supposed. Was he the guy?

I couldn't jump to conclusions.

I continued to study the area but didn't see anyone

else who looked remotely suspicious, nor did I see any DEA officers lurking undercover or waiting to strike. Only a mom with a toddler and an elderly woman with a cane.

Buttercup made eye contact with me, but quickly looked away, as if she didn't want to give any clues that she'd called me to anyone watching.

I casually went to the vitamin aisle again and began browsing the supplements there. As I did, I kept one eye on the situation at the pharmacy counter.

The olive-skinned man stood with a sigh and went to the counter. "I've been waiting for almost thirty minutes. Do you know when this will be ready?"

Buttercup shrugged. "Let me check."

She wandered to the pharmacist, they whispered something, and then she came back to the counter. "It's going to be another ten minutes."

"Then I'll have to come back later. I have an appointment I must get to. You're all usually much prompter than this, which is why I recommend people coming here. I guess that will have to change."

"Wait one minute, Mr. Stephens," the pharmacist called. "I'm almost done."

They were trying to stall until the DEA got here. My guess was that if this guy left now, he wouldn't be back.

I waited to see how everything would play out.

The man paced. Muttered beneath his breath. Checked his phone.

Time continued to tick away.

"It's been three minutes," he finally said. He didn't actually sound entirely rude—just irritated. I would be too if I was kept waiting this long. Provided I was also innocent of any crimes.

"I've got it right here." The pharmacist held up a bag.

I glanced around. There was still no sign of any DEA agents. Where were they? They should be here.

The pharmacist met the man at a little window and explained the medication. I could barely hear, but it sounded like it was some pain meds.

Mr. Stephens paid the bill and headed out.

I put my vitamin B down and cast a glance at Buttercup.

Her eyes were wide, like she wanted to say something. Most likely: Where was the DEA? Wasn't that the question all of us were thinking?

I didn't stick around to talk to Buttercup. No, I followed Mr. Stephens out the door. Casually. I hoped.

He climbed into the black Mercedes. And I climbed into the driver's seat of my blue Toyota.

"What happened?" Evie rushed.

I kept my eyes on that Mercedes. "I'm about to find out where this guy is heading. Maybe this will give us some answers."

I pulled out onto the street. Thankfully, it was winter so this part of Virginia Beach wasn't crazy busy like it got in the touristy summer season.

As I followed the man, I gave Evie and Sherman an update.

"He's turning!" Evie's arm stretched out in front of me, practically under my nose, as she pointed straight ahead.

Casually, I eased onto the road, following the Mercedes. Where in the world was he going? It was away from the resort area, which I thought was strange. I passed three other drugstores as I followed him. Why had he chosen the one he did instead of a closer location?

Unless he was involved in something illegal and thought a small, privately owned pharmacy would be easier to scam.

Which very well could be the case.

Eventually the resort area faded completely, and we headed toward a more rural, industrial part of town, an area dotted with old houses original to the area. The farmland had been invaded by warehouses and strings of shops every couple of miles.

Give it a few years and there would be entire new subdivisions in this area, if I had to guess. Developments had begun to overrun most of the city, and suburbia continued to expand and conquer everything in its path.

Five minutes later, the Mercedes pulled to a stop in front of a small line of shops. One sold farm supplies. Another was a kitchen and bath expo. I couldn't read what the faint words on the door in front of him said, and there was no sign above the building, only on the door.

I pulled to the side, behind another car, and watched.

The man got out of his vehicle, not looking frazzled in the least.

Which should mean that he hadn't seen me.

He walked toward the door of the building, pulled it open, and slipped inside.

"We've got to get closer!" Evie said.

"I'm trying," I said, feeling irritated. Of course, I was going to get closer. I just couldn't blow my cover in the process.

When I was sure Stephens was inside and he'd had a few minutes to settle, I pulled out of the parking space and crept toward the building.

When I was close enough to read the sign, I paused.

Wellington Adoption Agency.

An adoption agency?

What in the world?

"Any theories right about now?" I asked. I stared at the building, feeling dumbfounded.

This was one twist I hadn't seen coming.

Evie looked equally as baffled. "Maybe Brooke was considering being a surrogate mom."

"She couldn't conceive with her husband, and—I don't know what the issue was—but I'm hesitant to think that theory could be true," I murmured. "Maybe Brooke secretly wanted to adopt."

"So she came to an adoption agency without telling Conrad?" Sherman leaned toward the front seat, also staring at the building. "Sounds cold. And unhealthy."

"Or maybe Brooke did tell him, and he just didn't tell us." Evie cast me another I-told-you-so look.

"Good point." I wished Evie's theory wasn't a possibility, but it was. "Yet even if that was true, how would all of this have contributed to the fact that Brooke is missing?"

Evie leaned back in her seat and shook her head. "I have no idea."

"Me either," Sherman added.

I let out a sigh—both excited for a new lead and slightly exhausted. Had we been off track this whole time? I didn't even want to think about that. "Maybe this adoption agency and the whole prescription drug thing have nothing to do with Brooke."

"I don't know," Evie said. "All of this is fishy. That doctor was writing fraudulent prescriptions, probably with Brooke's assistance. One of the people receiving one of those prescriptions is somehow connected with this adoption agency. There could be something here. Maybe not with Brooke, but it sounds interesting either way."

I ran a hand over my forehead. "I think I'm getting a headache. But I am going back to one thing. What if

Brooke did secretly want to adopt? What if that somehow got her into this mess?"

"How would that work?" Sherman asked. "I'm having trouble connecting all the dots."

"I am too," I admitted. "Maybe Brooke created the patient profiles in exchange for the money that goes toward an adoption."

"We need to find out more about this agency." Evie's stone-cold gaze was laser focused on the building in front of us, like she now had a personal vendetta.

"How do we do that?" Sherman said. "You want me to hack into something?"

"Yes, but I also think someone needs to go undercover and pretend like they want to adopt from this Wellington agency." Evie turned toward me, a new gleam in her eyes. "You think Riley is up for it?"

"Riley?" I blinked in surprise, trying to picture it playing out. I was thankful I didn't have any coffee in my mouth because I might have spewed it out.

"Why not? You're married. You make more sense. Anyone would be able to tell that Sherman and I aren't a couple." She let out a snort, like the idea was absurd.

I cringed at the definitive and slightly demeaning sound of her voice. "I'm sure Riley would be game. If it means finding answers and helping his friend Conrad."

"Then we should go for it." Evie sounded incredibly certain and sure of herself.

"Should we stay here and try to follow this guy in the meantime?" Sherman asked.

I felt exhausted at the thought of it. Following this guy could mean being here for hours until he left. It sounded miserable. But if that's what we had to do, that's what we had to do. These long drawn-out wastes of time were harder when we only had a limited amount of days to get this done. We had to make the most of every moment. The trick was figuring out how to do that. Evie and Sherman were leaving in three days.

"I wish we'd driven separately," I muttered. "I don't feel like we're all needed for this. But, as they say, hindsight is twenty-twenty."

"How about if someone stays here and the others Uber back to pick up the other car?" Evie said.

"It's an idea." At least we'd use our time more effectively.

"It makes the most sense that you stay," Evie continued.

I bit back a sigh. "I guess you're right. I make the most sense to stay."

"It's settled then." Evie nodded and pulled out her phone. "I'll call Uber and get them to pick us up."

I glanced over at Evie, wondering if she planned on investigating her foster mom's disappearance more. "What are you guys going to do?"

Evie dialed a number and put her phone to her ear, not missing a beat. "We can keep researching the prescription drug fraud angle. We can also look into this Wellington Adoption Agency and see what we can find out."

It sounded like she had everything worked out. "While I wait, I'll call Conrad and see if he knows anything about this."

At least I had something to offer.

"We've got a plan," Evie said. "Let's get to it."

CHAPTER SEVENTEEN

Uber couldn't get here quickly enough, so Riley had to come pick Evie and Sherman up. He'd brought Sir Watson with him because Clarice had class and had to leave. After Riley left the dog with me, he was going to drop off my friends and go work out. I supposed it seemed like a good trade off.

We'd told Riley our plan—including his role—and everyone set out to complete their tasks.

And my task was to stay and keep my eyes on the Wellington Adoption Agency.

Which felt like a waste of time. Had I mentioned that? I hoped the payoff was worth it. Like, I really hoped it was worth it.

Evie and Sherman would have to leave on Saturday. I'd have to return to my part-time work. And I'd have to pick out paint colors. "What do you think, Watson?

Seafoam green for the living room? Or maybe a yellow? Misty day gray?"

Watson nuzzled my hand. He didn't seem to mind all of this. In fact, he seemed to be enjoying himself.

I didn't want to waste Garrett's money by investigating in this case, only for no answers to show for it. Or for Conrad to be guilty. Had he hired us, hoping to throw suspicion off himself?

I still had too many questions and not nearly enough answers.

I leaned back in my seat, stared at the adoption agency, and began to hash out my theories on how this might be connected with Brooke.

Or maybe the place wasn't connected at all, and this was just a wild goose chase. I didn't know, and I wouldn't know until I had more details. But I needed to explore the possibility that maybe Brooke had begun to look into adoption. What if she couldn't—or didn't want to—wait for in vitro? What if she'd gone on one of her spending sprees and begun this very expensive process? Could she have done that without Conrad's input?

I wouldn't think so. But if Brooke was sneaky enough, maybe. Had she posed as a single woman wanting a child?

I had a lot to think about.

Before I could think any longer, the man from the pharmacy exited the building. My heart rate spiked.

Yes! Maybe this was it—the part where I'd actually make some progress and not waste the rest of my day.

I put my car into drive. As soon as Stephens left the parking lot, I pulled out behind him. I maintained a respectable distance from his vehicle. I'd had enough experience to know not to get close and show my hand.

So far, I didn't think the man had a clue I was behind him.

But as he turned onto one of the main boulevards through Virginia Beach, traffic thickened. More than thickened. It was like rush hour on steroids. What in the world?

Then I remembered that one of the aircraft carriers had come into port in Norfolk today. That meant approximately five thousand extra people on the streets. You could tell a noticeable difference in the area.

I craned my neck around traffic, trying to keep my eye on the Mercedes. But as cars crowded around me, it was becoming harder. James Taylor's "Traffic Jam" began playing in my head.

Where was this Stephens guy heading? Who was he? Was he connected with Brooke? Or was this a wild goose chase?

I pressed on the accelerator, trying to keep the car in my sights. Just as I gained some distance, the light in front of me turned yellow.

I pressed the pedal harder and gripped the steering wheel.

I could do this. I could make it.

Just as I reached the light, the driver in front of me hit the brake.

I glanced to my left, ready to go around the car. But there were vehicles there.

On my right also.

I jammed my foot on my brake also.

My shoulders sagged as I watched as the Mercedes zoomed away.

I'd try to find him when the light turned. But I had little hope it would happen.

I dropped off Sir Watson at the house with Riley and then went to meet with Evie and Sherman at the hotel. Evie's suite had a little living area, where we gathered.

I had to admit that I was tired. Really tired. I just wanted to go home and think about how to handle all of this. I needed time to process and decompress and listen to my favorite songs. Maybe even watch *The Greatest Showman* again. Okay, actually for the sixth time. I was kind of obsessed.

Mainly, I hoped to listen and not really talk or theorize too much. Not for now.

Thankfully, Evie and Sherman seemed okay with that.

"I was able to see some of the hospital doctor's records," Sherman said, sitting on the edge of his orange-

and-green armchair, angled toward the computer in front of him.

"Did you cover your tracks?" I asked, still uncomfortable with the legal ramifications of his probing.

"Of course. No one will have a clue. Anyway, most of the prescriptions this guy doled out were for narcotics."

That wasn't surprising.

"But there were also a few prescriptions for a vitamin K injection and for erythromycin ointment." Sherman carefully watched my expression, looking rather pleased with himself.

"What is erythromycin ointment?" I asked, leaning back into the stiff couch and searching my mental vat of useless information for something that suddenly wasn't so useless.

His smile widened. "It's an eye ointment usually given to . . . newborns."

I let that sink in for a minute. "That's strange."

"I know."

"Of course, that could have been one of the legit scripts this doctor wrote," I said, trying to think everything through. "We don't know for sure, right?"

"I suppose we don't know. But at the hospital the doctor wouldn't have to write a script for it. They should have that at the hospital pharmacy. Doctors usually use it after babies are born."

The cold feeling in my gut grew colder, almost like the

cast from *Frozen* had taken up residence inside me. "I'm liking the case less and less all the time."

Something bad was going on here, and a happy ending was seeming less and less likely.

"There's something that's been bugging me lately as well." Evie pulled out a file from a stiff-sided briefcase beside her. That was Evie—always organized and on the ball. "I've been trying to do a profile on Brooke, and, the truth is, I just can't see her being a criminal."

"What do you mean?" My head felt like it was going to explode. These two had been busy—which was good but also overwhelming right now.

"I mean that Brooke doesn't fit the psychological profile of someone who is going to break the law." Evie now wore her smug look.

I was glad that finding this evidence was so satisfying to both of them. I could fault neither because I totally understood. There *was* something entirely satisfying about discovering new information and inching closer to the truth.

But there were still some other facts we needed to take into account. "Anyone can break the law," I argued.

"True. But Brooke was someone who looked out for others. She went back to school in order to earn money. She tried to make her wrongs right by getting a job in nursing. I don't think she's involved in anything illegal. She just doesn't fit the profile."

"I've seen good people do bad things plenty of times

before," I said. I wished that wasn't the case, but it was. All it took was one or two wrong choices, and a person's life and reputation could be damaged, sometimes irreversibly so. I'd seen it with my own eyes.

"I think that Brooke was set up," Evie announced, placing her hands on her lap with finality.

I rubbed my temples, that dull headache still present. "That's an interesting theory."

"You look tired. Go home. Sleep on it. And we'll talk again tomorrow."

I couldn't argue. That sounded like a great idea.

I couldn't wait to see Riley. And maybe even Sir Watson. And I needed to see if Riley had called the adoption agency. Knowing my luck, we couldn't get an appointment for another few months, which wouldn't help with this investigation.

But when I walked into my house, I noticed that something seemed different.

Riley stepped from the kitchen, a dewy bottle of water in his hands, and a smile on his face. "I have good news."

"What's that?" And where was—

"Sir Watson's owner came and picked him up."

My heart squeezed. "What?"

"Yeah, he saw the flyer and called right after you left. He showed up here ten minutes later, and the two were reunited."

"Oh . . . that's great." That was what I'd wanted, right? For Sir Watson to go home?

Riley stepped closer, a wrinkle between his eyebrows. "Why do you look sad?"

"I guess I just thought I'd be able to tell him goodbye."

Riley squeezed my arm in a mild—albeit confused—attempt at comfort. "I'm sorry, Gabby. I didn't think you even liked him."

"I don't . . . I didn't. I mean, it doesn't really matter anymore, right?" I was confusing myself, so I had little hope this would make sense to anyone else.

"You *did* like Sir Watson." Riley grinned as realization washed over him. "You really liked him, maybe you just didn't know it."

I shrugged, not ready to fully acknowledge he was correct. "Maybe I did a little. Did he seem happy?"

"The owner?"

"No, Watson." Of *course.*

Riley shrugged and stepped back. "I guess. I mean, I don't know. It was a little weird. The man brought one of Watson's favorite treats with him, so Watson liked that. It was actually fresh steak."

Fresh steak? What kind of person brought fresh steak to pick up their dog? Someone who wanted to entice the dog away? Who wanted to instantly earn the dog's trust?

No, I was reading too much into this. There wasn't a crime around every corner or in every act. I'd been tainted.

"Oh, and get this. The dog's real name is Stephens."

"Stephens?" My heart skipped a beat.

"Is something wrong with that?"

My mind raced. Was I being irrational? Or brilliantly insightful? "No, it's just that . . . that's the last name of someone I'm investigating. This man didn't have dark hair and wear a suit, did he?"

"No, he didn't."

I let out a little laugh. "I'm just seeing mysteries where there aren't any, I suppose."

"Oh, and I have other good news," Riley continued. "That adoption agency had a cancelation for tomorrow morning. We're in."

CHAPTER EIGHTEEN

The next morning, I stared at myself in the full-length bedroom mirror and frowned.

I'd spent a considerable amount of time picking out what to wear to this interview. I didn't want it to be too casual—then they might not take me seriously. Nor did I want to look too professional—they might not think I was ready for motherhood.

Instead, I'd chosen some neat jeans, a respectable-looking light-blue shirt, and flats. Overall, I thought it had a good mommy vibe going.

But my spirit felt unsettled—especially when I thought about Sir Watson. Was the dog okay? Was that really his owner who picked him up?

Of course it was, I mentally scoffed. Why would someone else take him?

Riley appeared in the reflection behind me, wrapped

his arms around my waist, and waited until my gaze met his. "You ready for this?"

I turned around to face him and soaked in the burgundy-colored Henley he wore. It brought out the warmth in his skin tones and made his eyes sparkle. "I suppose I'm ready. How about you?"

"Whatever I can do to help," he said.

I smiled. This was a change from the start of our relationship when Riley had encouraged me not to get involved in any investigation. I supposed he'd given up and accepted that this was my calling in life. Or maybe nearly losing his life had made him realize that time was too short to be afraid of doing what you loved.

"Then let's go." I took his hand and pulled him into the living room. "And remember, when possible, let's stick to the truth."

We'd already gone over our cover story several times.

Before we left, I turned and looked at Sir Watson's kennel. It didn't seem right that it sat there empty. I'd even formulated a way to use a carabiner to keep the mutt in his cage when I went to work.

Then I'd woken up and remembered he was gone.

"You were really good with Sir Watson, you know," I said.

"I don't know that I'd say that. I was doing what makes sense."

Riley held the door open for me, and I stepped out.

"You're going to be like that as a dad too, aren't you?"

I continued. "You'll be one of those people to whom parenting comes naturally, and you're going to make it look easy."

"I'm sure parenting isn't easy."

I paused on the porch and glanced around. Was anyone watching me? I didn't see anyone suspicious.

But that unsettled feeling in my gut remained.

"I know—and that's my point," I continued. "You're going to make it look easy."

"I keep trying to figure out if you're complimenting or insulting me." He cast me a confused look. "Your words sound like a compliment, but your tone sounds like an insult."

I released my breath. "It's a compliment. I'm just jealous."

"Don't be jealous. I'm sure you'll be a great mom one day."

"I wish I felt that certain." Perhaps growing up in a dysfunctional home had tainted my view. Perhaps I feared following in my parents' footsteps. I wasn't sure.

But pretending like I wanted to adopt was playing with my head. And I didn't like it one bit.

Riley and I pulled up to the Wellington Adoption Agency twenty minutes later. While we were there, Evie and Sherman were going to follow up on that dead body that was found in the woods, look into Mr. Abe's background, and possibly tail Conrad again.

My hands trembled as we walked up to the agency's door. Even Riley murmuring in my ear that everything was going to be okay didn't calm me, nor did the inviting sunlight that warmed the otherwise cool day.

Something about this whole setup had shaken me.

For example—what did an adoption agency have to do with this whole mess? I wasn't even sure I wanted to find out, because the possibilities seemed too atrocious for me to comprehend. Using kids—or people's desire for kids—as a part of any kind of criminal activity was wrong on so many levels. But I also needed to consider that maybe this was legit.

An older woman with a poof of fragile blonde hair and a congenial smile greeted us from behind the front desk. "Good morning! We're so glad you could be here with us today. You must be the Thomases."

"That's us," I said with more enthusiasm than I felt.

"Wonderful. Well, we have some paperwork for you to fill out first before you meet with one of our counselors. Hopefully, they warned you that the paperwork—and application process—is quite extensive. It can overwhelm some people. They also told you about the five thousand-dollar processing fee?"

I blanched. No, they hadn't mentioned that. Five thousand dollars? Just to go through this orientation process?

I felt slightly lightheaded.

"It's no problem." Riley pulled out his wallet.

Of course, Garrett would reimburse us this expense since it was for the investigation. I just hoped we had enough in our checking account to cover it in the meantime. Riley handed the woman our credit card, and she inserted it into a machine. Once we had it back, we were dismissed to begin the paperwork.

As I sat down in a comfortable chair against the wall in the waiting area, I glanced around. Pictures of smiling families with children were all around me.

My heart panged at their sweet, innocent faces.

I didn't think I was ready for children. But maybe part of me was. Maybe part of me did want to take that next step.

The thought surprised even me.

"How about you start with these, and I'll fill in our family profile?" Riley asked, handing me part of the paperwork.

I pulled myself from my thoughts and glanced at Riley, snapping back to reality. "Yes. Of course, honey."

I took the packet and began answering all the many, many questions. By the time I finished, my hand hurt, as well as my head. And it seemed like a shame to do all this work and not actually adopt.

When I saw the section where I needed to give references, I paused. This was going to prove difficult . . . since I hadn't gotten approval from anyone yet to give their name, nor had I informed them of what we were doing.

Despite that, I jotted down our pastor's name. Garrett's name. And Sierra's.

I really hoped this didn't go far enough that they'd call any of those people. The rumors that would start . . .

A fine sweat covered my forehead as I continued.

Thirty minutes later, Riley and I finished, handed in our paperwork, and were escorted to a room in the back where a smiling man greeted us.

It was the man I'd seen yesterday. Mr. Stephens. He wore a suit again today and looked respectable and professional.

"Mr. and Mrs. Thomas," he said. "I'm Joseph Stephens. It's a pleasure to meet you."

Our file sat in front of him. He'd used the same name here as he had at the pharmacy. That was a good sign . . . probably.

We returned the pleasantries.

"You both look a little nervous. There's nothing unusual about that. This is a big step." He leaned back. "If you don't mind, I like to start this interview process with some basics. How long have you known you wanted to adopt?"

Riley nodded at me, so I took the lead. I'd already gone over this story in my mind, and I'd decided that it would be better if we sounded desperate to adopt instead of led to adopt, if that made sense. Criminals preyed on desperate people, and we needed to make ourselves look like a target right now.

"We've been married for almost a year but together for much longer," I started, squeezing Riley's hand and trying to stick to the truth as much as possible. "But I've known since I was a teenager that I'd be unable to have children."

"I'm sorry to hear that."

I glanced at my hands. "I'd hoped the doctors were wrong. I mean, you hear stories about that all the time, right? Women who are told they're infertile but then one day—surprise! They're pregnant. Unfortunately, I don't believe that will be our story."

The man's eyes softened with compassion. "Yes, I've heard that before. You're not alone."

"We're ready to take the next step and have a family of our own," Riley added, squeezing my hand.

Riley's words threw me off for a moment. He'd almost sounded sincere. But he was just acting. He was better at this than I'd thought.

"Well, you've come to the right place. We've successfully helped hundreds of families become families. And it just so happens that we have many willing birth moms right now."

I swallowed hard. Willing birth moms? It wasn't like these women were giving blood. They'd made the brave choice to give their child a different future. Something about how he said those words didn't settle right with me.

"Willing birth moms?" I repeated.

Joseph nodded. "That's right. We strictly use mothers

who, for one reason or another, want to give their babies up for adoption. It's a very brave decision, and we counsel them extensively to make sure this is really what they want to do. Because of this, we're able to match families with newborns so the bonding can begin right away."

I had to admit, he made adoption sound very exciting. For a moment, this felt real. I reminded myself that it wasn't.

"Before we go too far, we do have to ensure that you have the funding in place," he said. "We usually ask that adoptive families pay for the birth mother's medical expenses. There are programs in place to help you raise money, but that will delay the amount of time it will take to get the ball rolling, so to speak."

"We're prepared to begin right away and use money from our savings," Riley said. "We can verify we have the funds to cover all the expenses."

The man's eyes lit up. "Great. We'll need to set up a home study, as well as . . ."

As he continued, my mind drifted.

Had Brooke done this? Sat in this seat? Had it been with hope in her heart? Or had she been devising a scheme—either to profit herself or to reconcile with Conrad?

I honestly had no idea.

CHAPTER NINETEEN

Riley and I left the adoption agency three hours later, and to say I was mentally exhausted would be an understatement. Joseph Stephens had asked so many questions. So. Many. Questions.

My head was spinning. What kind of mom did I think I would be? How many children did I want? Would I be willing to accept a child with a medical condition? Or of a different race?

And Riley and I weren't done with this yet. No, right now, we were going to try and tail Joseph again.

Until he left, Riley and I would sit in our car and wait.

"Phase one is done," Riley murmured, his hand on the small of my back.

"My brain needs a massage now."

He chuckled. "It was . . . intense."

I just hoped Joseph Stephens wasn't here for hours

upon hours. Had I mentioned how much I'd come to despise stakeouts yet?

As we stepped out the door, I gasped and drew back. Another couple stood there, about to enter the agency. They were probably in their late thirties, but their gaze looked cautiously hopeful as they held hands and smiled apologetically.

"I'm so sorry," I told them. "I was in my own little world and didn't even see you."

The man—a ginger probably twenty pounds over-weight—nodded. "It's no problem."

We took another step away when the woman said, "Excuse me."

Riley and I paused and turned.

The woman glanced at her husband—I assumed that's who he was—before continuing. "I know this is nosy, but have you adopted from Wellington already?"

Riley casually rested his hands in his pockets. "We're just starting the process."

"So are we." The woman's voice sounded tight with anticipation. "We're giddy excited about the possibility of adding to our family. Our friends just adopted from a different agency—they don't live in this area. I was just wondering if you'd had a good experience."

"I'd love to give you more feedback, but it's too early to say," Riley told her. "We started the application process only this morning."

"I know it's expensive." The woman's smile dimmed,

and she glanced at her husband. "We had to refinance our house. But it will be worth it to hold a little one in our arms. We aren't able to have children on our own. We've been trying for seven years. Even did the whole in vitro route. We finally realized it was time to move on."

My heart panged with compassion. I could tell by her voice that their journey had been painful and tinged with heartache. "I'm glad you found Wellington, then."

Unless Wellington proved to be some sort of scam.

Then my heart just panged with grief for the whole situation. For hopeful parents whose expectations had risen with excitement. Who'd emptied their life savings. Who thought they'd reached their dreams.

Hope deferred makes the heart sick, but a longing fulfilled is a tree of life. Proverbs 12:12. The verse made more sense now than ever.

"I hope everything goes well," I finally said.

Putting a face to more potential victims only made my heart sick, though. My gut feeling was that this investigation was bigger than Brooke. The implications were more far-reaching.

Riley and I climbed into our car and sat together for a moment in silence.

"I hope that couple doesn't get caught up in some kind of scam," Riley finally said.

"Me too. They seemed nice."

Riley turned toward me, a new somberness washing over him. "What do you think about the agency?"

"They could be legit," I said, not sounding convincing even to myself. "I mean, that man—Mr. Stephens—could have been picking up that medication at the pharmacy for his personal use. Maybe this case has nothing to do with the adoptions themselves."

Again, I wished I believed my own words. But I didn't.

"It is a possibility," Riley said. "We're just skimming the surface of this now."

I leaned back and sighed. "I can see why the case went cold. There's just no strong evidence to indicate what happened to Brooke."

Riley squeezed my knee and left his hand resting there. "You'll figure it out."

"I'm not so sure." And I really didn't like failing. I didn't like it one bit. "Usually at this point in an investigation, I would at least have an inkling of what might have happened—even if I'm wrong. In this case, I'm clueless. I thought maybe Brooke was doing something illegal with prescription drugs. That led me to this adoption agency— but they appear legit. Maybe this has been one rabbit trail after another."

A lull in the conversation stretched between us until Riley asked, "What do you think about adoption?"

I blinked at Riley's question. We hadn't really talked about this much. I assumed we'd hash things out when we reached that point one day. "I . . . I don't know. I always assumed I'd be fruitful and multiply the old-fash-ioned way. But I wouldn't be opposed to adoption."

"I guess it doesn't really matter right now, does it?" Riley said, staring out the window. "Neither of us are ready to have kids."

I nodded, relief flushing through me. "Right. I mean, totally."

A small part of me had been thinking about it more lately. Mostly when I saw Sierra with Reef, but I tried to brush it off.

I couldn't quite identify what this restlessness inside me was.

Was something internal urging me to look for a new job? Maybe.

Or perhaps I had the urge to make sure I made the most of my life, to not just mosey along, comfortable with the status quo.

I didn't know. But I hated the way my stomach clenched.

Riley sat up straight and nodded in the distance. "Look at that."

I followed his gaze in time to see someone leaving the building.

It wasn't Mr. Stephens.

No, I squinted to get a better look at the man. Part of his face looked like . . . it had been scarred in a fire.

A whoosh of realization flushed through me. "He's the

one who came into the hospital to see Brooke, who looked through their mail."

"He's also Watson's owner," Riley muttered.

I swung my head toward him, certain I'd heard him incorrectly. "What?"

"That's the man who came to pick up the dog yesterday."

My gut feeling hadn't been off. Someone had taken Sir Watson. Someone linked with this investigation. But why would he do that?

CHAPTER TWENTY

"Don't lose him!" My gaze fastened on the truck in front of us.

"I've got this," Riley said.

The way he said it totally made me believe him.

"Why would that man take Sir Watson?" I murmured, still in disbelief that that dog was connected with this mess.

But something had sounded fishy to me from the start about Sir Watson's supposed owner. What kind of owner brought steak with him to pick up his dog?

"I don't know, Gabby." Riley pulled onto another street, continuing to tail the black, mid-sized truck. "Maybe he was trying to feel us out. Maybe he wanted to scope out our house, our lives."

That sounded right. But . . . "What did he do with Sir Watson afterward?"

Riley frowned. "I . . . I don't know. I wish I did."

Emotion clogged my throat. I should have been there. I should have stopped this.

Except that man had probably been watching me. He'd probably moved in after I left—on purpose.

That also meant that he knew I was investigating him. Somewhere along the line, I'd hit on something connected with Brooke's disappearance. All of this wasn't a wild goose chase.

The fact filled me with relief.

But also caution.

When had I shown my hand? To whom? I needed to think this through. I'd do that more later. Right now, we needed to follow this guy and see where he was going.

It wasn't rush hour this time—that was the good news. But it also meant we needed to be more careful about not being spotted since there weren't as many cars to conceal us.

"I don't really like where this is going." Riley gripped the steering wheel harder.

"But that man proves a link between Brooke and this whole prescription-slash-adoption investigation. The pieces are all there, Riley. I just need to figure out how to put them together."

He pulled into another lane as we merged onto the interstate. "Tell me the pieces again."

I ticked off the facts on my fingers. "Brooke is a nurse who's in debt and who wants kids. She's most likely involved in a prescription drug scheme. One of the men who was prescribed these drugs—and who is possibly in on the scheme—just happens to work at an adoption agency. The man who was possibly stalking Brooke and who claimed Sir Watson is also hanging out at thus-said agency."

Riley's jaw flexed as he seemed to process it all. "So, a missing woman. Drug fraud. Adoption. I don't know what this all means, but I don't like the sound of it."

"Me either."

"I do feel like you're on the verge of putting this all together." Riley pulled in and out of traffic, still following the man.

Scarface was headed away from the Virginia Beach oceanfront area and toward Norfolk.

As the man took an exit, Riley veered from the interstate and followed him toward downtown Norfolk. We continued to follow him until he slowed near . . . an area of stacked cargo containers?

What?

"I'd say this was a port, but we're not even by the water," I muttered.

"There are train tracks, though. My guess is they load these containers onto trains, and those trains might take these containers to the port."

But what was in those big metal boxes? And how did they tie in with the case? Or did they?

There was no guard at the front, just an iron gate that

probably got locked up at night—which would make spying on this guy a little easier.

"I say we pull over and do the rest of this on foot." I released my seatbelt.

Sneaking around containers stacked three or four high seemed like something that happened in every action adventure movie. Traveling through the maze of metal was pretty unnerving in real life, however.

I felt small. As if I could be in a new book as part of the *Maze Runner* series. As if the mafia or another group of bad guys might find us at any minute and stuff us into one of these oversized boxes before shipping us overseas.

Unrealistic? Maybe.

But the fear was still real.

Riley held my hand, his grip tight and firm as we scrambled around, trying to locate the truck without being seen. There must be at least ten rows of containers, each stacked three or four high with probably twenty stacks per row.

As voices carried across the wind toward us, we paused at the edge of a rusty orange cargo box.

Riley put a finger over his lips. Which was adorable. Like I didn't know I had to stay quiet.

I strained my ears, trying to make out what was being said.

"Is everything set for Friday?" someone—Scarface?—asked.

I wanted to peer around the corner and see whom he

was talking to. But I couldn't risk it. Instead, I continued to listen.

"We're good to go," someone else said. "You bring the goods, we'll load them, and another part of our plan will be considered a success."

"You sure this is going to work?"

"We've done it once before," the other man said. "No one's going to talk. Not with everything that's at stake."

Footsteps sounded. Coming our way. My heartbeat kicked up a notch.

We couldn't let these guys find us.

Riley tugged my arm. He pulled me away from the edge and around the corner. Out of sight.

I pressed myself into the cool metal, hardly able to get a good, deep breath. I listened. Footsteps and low, murmuring voices continued to head this way.

Riley and I exchanged a look. Slowly, we crept back farther. He peered around another corner before motioning that I should follow.

We slipped out of sight just as the men walked past.

I released my breath.

That had been close. We'd almost been caught, and my fears might have become reality.

I didn't know what was going on here, but whatever it was, it wasn't good.

And just what did Brooke have to do with it all?

CHAPTER TWENTY-ONE

After I dropped Riley off, I met with Evie and Sherman at their hotel and gave them the update. Then I waited anxiously to hear what they'd learned.

"Mr. Abe, as you call him, did go to jail for six months for supposedly watching his neighbor," Sherman started, popping a potato chip into his mouth as he stared at the notes he'd scribbled on a yellow legal pad. "He was only twenty-one at the time, and he's had no incidences since then."

"So maybe he is a good guy who either got a bad rap or made a bad choice," I said, suddenly hungry as I watched my friend munch on deep-fried, salty goodness.

"Maybe," Evie said. She eyeballed Sherman also, but it wasn't in an envious manner. No, she looked annoyed as she picked up a grape and ate it.

The two had obviously hit up the deli downstairs.

"We also looked into the dead woman who was found yesterday," Evie continued. "The body hasn't been identified, but doesn't appear to be Brooke. The official description fits her physically, but the woman was a mother, from what I heard."

"How did you hear that? Is it public?" I asked, curious as to how they'd gotten that information.

Evie and Sherman exchanged a look.

"Not exactly," Evie said, eating another grape. "But we were able to learn where the medical examiner hangs out. It's this great little smoothie bar. We overheard part of the conversation."

"And I creatively obtained the rest." Sherman crumpled his bag and threw it into the trashcan in the corner.

He'd hacked, in other words. We could seriously get into trouble for this. Yet part of me didn't want to stop.

"It also appears the woman died several months ago," Evie said.

"Define 'several.'"

Evie shifted, crossing her legs at the ankles. "We're not sure, but I'd guess at least four or five."

I let that sink in a moment. I wasn't sure if it meant anything or not, but I would keep it in the back of my mind. I tucked my own leg beneath me on the couch where I sat. "Anything else?"

"I looked into Wellington Adoption Agency," Sherman said, picking up his notepad. "They have rave reviews.

Everyone who's worked with them speaks highly of the experience."

"Those are the people who ended up with children," I said. "I guess that does make them happy."

"There was one person who left a bad review. I guess their adoption fell through at the last minute," Evie said. "We're trying to get in touch with this couple and find out more information, but we haven't had any luck yet."

"Sounds like you did good work," I said. Maybe working with a team did have its benefits. I just needed to remind myself of that next time I was presented with another cold case.

"We did a lot of that while sitting outside Conrad's school," Sherman said. "He didn't leave. Again. It looks like that lead is futile."

"The school would have to record it if he left during school hours," I said. "It would be a red flag to the police if he did. Certainly authorities are monitoring that."

"You're probably right," Evie said.

I stared at Evie a minute, trying to read her pensive expression. I couldn't really understand what was going on inside her head. Even though my first impulse was simply to be annoyed, something urged me to not give up on her. The woman was complex, to say the least.

"Any more leads on your foster mom?" I asked, stealing one of her grapes and eating it before she could stop me.

She frowned and gave me a look before her gaze

turned stormy. "No, I haven't looked into that lately either. I will some more when I get back to Texas."

"I see. I hope you find answers." I meant those words. Living with unanswered questions could be like swimming toward the surface but feeling like you were never going to reach it, that your air would run out first.

Evie's gaze locked with mine. "I hope we all find answers."

When I got home that evening—to an empty home without Sir Watson—my phone rang. I sat on the couch and looked at the screen. I didn't recognize the number, but I answered anyway.

It was Macy.

"Hey, I was hoping I'd catch you," she said. "Listen, something just happened that you need to know about. Can we meet?"

Meeting was the last thing I wanted to do now. But her voice sounded urgent. "Is this about Brooke?"

"That's what I'm trying to figure out."

I hoped this didn't prove to be another waste of time. I needed clues that had sustenance. I needed answers.

But first I'd need to talk to Macy to figure out if this was legit or not. "Of course. Name the place."

She picked a little coffee shop near the hospital. I

pulled in there twenty minutes later and found Macy sitting at a table in the back.

The place was small, but the acoustic music overhead was fairly loud, which should help keep our conversation private. I bypassed getting a drink—I didn't need the caffeine—and went straight to Macy, who was nursing some tea, it appeared.

She looked like she'd come straight from work. She still wore her pink hospital scrubs, and her hair was in a neat ponytail. Her movements, however, were quick and almost anxious.

My curiosity grew, and my exhaustion seemed to fade. I paused to do something I should have been doing all along.

Praying.

Please give me wisdom here, God. I want to find answers for everyone. People need closure. Please guide my thoughts and help me to solve this, not for my glory but for the comfort of others.

After a silent "amen," I slid into the seat across from her and wasted no time in getting to the point. "What's going on?"

Macy's gaze flickered behind me, almost like she thought I might be watched. "I don't know if this has anything to do with Brooke or not. But I'm afraid it might, and I didn't know who to tell."

She had my full attention. "Go on."

"First, you have to promise not to tell the police." She stared at me, her gaze unwavering as she waited for my reaction to her ultimatum.

I folded my hands in front of me, trying to tap into some of that patience and wisdom I'd prayed for. "It's hard to promise that before I know what you're going to tell me. The cops are already on my case about being involved when they've made the investigation active again."

"Then I can't share the information." The final sound of Macy's words left no room for question, as did her crossed arms and pressed lips.

I leaned back, frustration mounting in me. I didn't come all the way here not to get any information. But I didn't want to put my reputation on the line either—especially since I had no idea what Macy was about to say or if the payoff would be worth it.

But what was more important—Brooke's life or my reputation?

I knew the answer. Clearly. Undoubtedly.

This wasn't about me. Investigations never were.

I let out a breath, a new wave of peace coming over me. "Okay, I'll keep this between us."

She also released a breath, and her shoulders seemed to relax. She leaned toward me and lowered her voice. "Someone approached me today about a job."

Okay, this had the potential to be good. I was

assuming Macy wouldn't tell me this unless she thought it might be connected with Brooke.

"Go on," I said.

Macy licked her lips before launching into the next part. "This man didn't give me very many details. Just said it was lucrative and part-time."

"Where did this guy find you?"

"In the parking lot of the hospital when I went out for my break."

Catching someone outside their place of employment? Didn't seem like that was on the up and up. "And did he give any details?"

Macy rubbed the side of her ceramic mug. "He just said his company needed people who were trained in the medical field. I think he thought I was a nurse. People get that wrong all the time."

"Did you correct him?" I watched her expression carefully.

Macy didn't even flinch. "No, because I thought this might be a lead. I decided I should probably go with it."

Probably a good idea. "Have you ever seen this man before?"

She shook her head again. "No, I haven't. Well . . . I take that back. He did look a little like a man who came into Labor and Delivery a couple weeks ago. His wife was having a baby. Or maybe it was his sister. I'm not really sure."

"What did he look like?" Maybe we were finally onto something. Maybe! Excitement coursed through me.

"He was tall with dark hair and an olive complexion."

Could that be Joseph Stephens? From the adoption agency? Maybe.

But I had more questions. "If this was a legit job, why not just advertise it? Why would he need to covertly sneak around and ask hospital employees as they left work?"

I didn't expect her to know the answer, but I wanted to voice the question aloud anyway.

"I asked him that," Macy said. "He said they only like to recruit the best, and they'd had too many subpar employees when they opened applications to the public."

I supposed it might be reasonable. I mentally gave Macy kudos for thinking to ask.

"What did you tell him?" I asked.

"I told him I'd meet him for the interview. I figured this might be our chance to figure out what happened to Brooke, and I didn't want it to pass. But I'm not sure if I did the right thing or not. It seemed like a good idea at the time." Her voice became more high-pitched. Her words came out faster. Her breaths were shallow.

"No, this could be a good thing. When are you meeting him? And where?"

"I'm supposed to meet tomorrow morning at nine. He mentioned a coffee shop that's inside a local grocery store.

He thought it might be more central. Also, I'm not meeting him—he's just a recruiter. I'm meeting his boss."

Unexpected, but okay . . . "Last question—you made me promise not to bring the police into this. Why?"

Macy's gaze locked onto mine. "Because when the man left me, he walked over to a car where another man was waiting. He was wearing a police uniform."

CHAPTER TWENTY-TWO

I had to let Macy's words sink in for a minute. A long minute. Okay, actually for an hour after I left Macy at the coffee house.

Could the police be in on whatever was going on? I didn't know.

But her news left me in an interesting situation.

Macy had said the man she'd seen had dark skin, was tall, and he looked tired. Could it have been Detective Belfield? Could he be involved in all of this? I didn't want to believe it. But I needed to consider the possibility.

I couldn't trust the wrong person. Not if I wanted to figure this all out.

I glanced around my living room. Riley was here, along with Evie and Sherman. They sat on the folding chairs from my temporary dining room table—since my couch cushions had been demolished.

I didn't have much time to formulate a plan, so I'd asked them to come right away.

"I need to disguise myself as Macy and go to meet this man," I announced.

Riley swung his head back and forth, his features painted with resistance. "It sounds like a bad, bad idea. So much could go wrong."

Though I agreed with him that so much could go wrong, I had to weigh the benefits and the risks. "This might be my only chance to find Brooke."

Riley's eyes narrowed. "Or you might go missing just like Brooke. You should tell the police."

I threw my hands in the air as I stood in front of the group, feeling almost like an attorney pleading my client's case to a jury of my peers. "They could be involved. Besides, this is a public space where we're supposed to meet. There are a lot of safety precautions already in place."

Riley remained quiet a moment before saying, "You don't look like Macy—not as you've described her to me, at least."

"I have a wig," I said. "Remember that costume party we went to last month for your office?"

They'd done a President's Day theme, so I'd dressed like Marilyn Monroe.

Riley nodded, but it looked begrudging. "I do."

"Besides, the person Macy is supposed to meet with hasn't actually seen her face up close. I mean, he thinks Macy is a nurse, so he's obviously not very educated."

"We'll be there to watch her back," Evie added. "As long as Gabby doesn't go anywhere with this guy, she should be okay. She could just gather information."

Riley crossed his arms, his gaze jumping from each of us like he was on the job and assessing the jury pool. "I still don't like this."

"None of us do," Sherman said. "I wish this was something I could simply solve by looking on the Internet. But it's not that easy."

Riley uncrossed his arms, obviously still not comfortable with this. "If you're going to do this, you better find some scrubs. And we don't have much time."

A burst of joy shot through me, and I threw my arms around him. "Thank you."

"Please be careful," he murmured. "I have a bad feeling about this."

I didn't know how this would turn out. But I wanted to find answers. I wanted to find Brooke. And, surprisingly, I wanted to find Sir Watson.

It seemed weird that the man doing this interview had asked to meet in a coffee shop that was a part of a huge grocery store. But I supposed there were worse places to meet. I mean, at least we were out in public here.

I had to drive myself, just in case anyone was watching. Evie and Sherman were already here at the store and pretending to be shoppers. They'd stay close by. Riley would arrive a few minutes after me. He'd get a cup of coffee and linger nearby as well.

I'd be lying if I didn't say I was as nervous as a tone-deaf musical director on opening night. The wig I wore was kind of itchy. Blonde wasn't my color. And I felt self-conscious in the pink scrubs, like everyone would look at me and know I wasn't cut out for the healthcare field. I'd much rather clean up after a dead person than give a living person a bath.

Despite that, I pushed forward. Why? Because that was what I did. It was what I *had* to do to reach my goals.

The coffee area at the grocery store was located in the front corner, a good thirty feet from the automatic door where I could exit. It had five little tables set up around the perimeter. I scanned the people there before my gaze stopped on a man with light brown hair who wore a suit.

That was him. The man I would meet with. My gut told me so.

I bypassed getting a drink. I'd probably only get nervous and spill it on myself anyway. Instead, I plastered on my best smile and approached the man.

Me again, God. I could use more wisdom here. I don't know what's going on, but I know people are getting hurt and deceived. That's what my gut tells me. Please help me to find some answers.

"Hi, there," I started. "I'm Macy. Are you waiting to meet someone?"

The man straightened, smiled, and extended his hand. "I am. I'm Devin Black. Thanks for meeting with me."

"I have to admit that I'm intrigued."

"I know this may seem unconventional, so thank you for meeting with me. Can I get you something to drink?"

"No, I'm fine. If I have any more caffeine or sugar, I'll be bouncing off the walls." *Or I'll throw up.* I didn't say that part.

The murmur of nearby shoppers filled the air, along with the sound of an overhead TV playing a news station. A heat vent above me felt overbearing. I wasn't sure if I was sweating because of my nerves or from the warm air pouring out. Maybe both.

"I know your shifts as a nurse can be exhausting." Devin offered a brief smile, the epitome of a nice, professional man from his mannerisms all the way to his suit and neat hair.

"You can say that again." I shifted, trying to gracefully steer the conversation back into helpful territory. "Speaking of which, how did you find me? I mean, I didn't exactly send out any applications."

"We're very selective in whom we ask to come onboard with us," he explained. "We ask for recommendations from people who've been patients at the hospital. That's one way."

"I see." I laced my hands together, trying not to show my nerves. "So what kind of job are we talking about?"

"You're direct and to the point." He smiled again, this time showing a flash of white.

I'd expected his teeth to be pearly white and straight, but instead they were slightly yellow and overlapping. Did that mean anything? I wasn't sure.

People could fix a lot of things about their appearance. But teeth were something that took a lot of time and finances. Changing them wasn't instantaneous, which was why dental records could say so much about a person's financial standing.

"I like that," he continued. "So I'll be direct and to the point with you."

I glanced over and saw Riley in line at the coffee counter. No one else would have noticed that he was watching me, but I did. He was looking at me out of the corner of his eye. And I was grateful to have someone watching my back.

I was certain Evie and Sherman were also close, but I didn't dare to look for them.

Devin pushed a set of papers toward me. I flipped past the cover page and stared at the information there.

"We help underprivileged women who are pregnant," Devin explained. "We offer prenatal care, as well as help with birth, delivery, and setting up their homes afterward, making sure both mother and baby are taken care of."

"Sounds reputable." Or totally reprehensible, depending. I knew one thing—I didn't like where this was going.

"I know this is a bit strange. But I assure you we're trustworthy. We've been in business for the past five years, and we've helped countless young women."

"What are the hours?"

"We work around your schedule. We don't expect anyone to give up their full-time job. And, quite frankly, we'd rather hire part-timers. That way, we can handle health care for our mothers instead of worrying about full-time employees."

He sounded so convincing. Then again, most swindlers did. Was he convincing low-income women to give up their babies? What about the prescription drugs? How did they fit in?

I touched my hair, still not used to the stiff strands of the blonde wig atop my head. My scalp itched from wearing it, but I resisted the urge to scratch. "I see. Forgive my questions, but I need to make sure this is on the up and up. How is this business even funded? It sounds quite costly."

"It's privately funded." The words rolled off his tongue, almost like he'd said them a million times before. "We have a fundraising team that takes care of all of this."

"Sounds like you have your act together." *Or should I say, scheme?*

"We like to think so. Our problem is that we're short right now a couple of nurses who will help to offer support to our clients. Does this sound like something you might be interested in?" He stared at me and waited, perfectly pleasant and still.

"I have to admit that I could use the extra cash."

"Most of us can."

I licked my lips. "What's the next step?"

Devin's eyes glowed with warmth. This man was a salesman, and he was good at his job. That was what made all of this even more sickening.

"Well, the regular forms have to be filled out as a matter of record," he said. "After we process those, we can officially offer you a job and set up your hours."

I nodded, certain to sound totally engaged. "Let's do it."

A story on the news caught my ear. It was hard to hear, but it sounded like the body in the woods had been iden-tified. Did the news anchor just say that the woman had been . . . a nurse?

The sick feeling in my stomach grew. Was she connected with all of this? I wasn't sure—that conclusion might be a stretch—but to say I was uneasy was an under-statement.

"I was hoping you'd say that." Devin must not have heard the news story because he seemed unaffected. "We're so happy to have you on board."

I forced a stiff smile "Me too."

Devin reached into his briefcase and frowned. "Some-how, those forms must have gotten left out in my car. Let me run and get them. I figured it was too good to be true that I'd covered all the bases. I've had quite the morning. My three-month-old has an ear infection and has only been sleeping for an hour at a time."

Good. He hadn't asked me to go with him. Maybe this would be easier than I thought.

And he'd mentioned having a baby. That made him seem more trustworthy. Smooth move.

Just as he stood up, a ringing filled the air.

The fire alarm, I realized. I looked up and saw smoke filling the back of the building.

A couple of employees began yelling that everyone needed to evacuate.

People abandoned their shopping carts and rushed toward the exit.

Everything had just gotten a little more interesting.

CHAPTER TWENTY-THREE

"I saw him do it!" a middle-aged woman screeched. "He started the fire over by the paper products."

My eyes followed the line of her arm and index finger.

My heart rate ricocheted when I saw she was pointing at Riley, as he stood there at the coffee pickup counter. Riley's eyes widened, and he drew his chin back, as if shocked.

This was a misunderstanding. Riley would explain that and walk away. And this would be over.

Still, my heart raced with anticipation.

I took a step toward Riley, nearly ready to break my cover, when a security guard grabbed his arm. "Come with me."

Riley glanced back at me, something close to panic in

his gaze. "No, you don't understand. I didn't have anything to do with this."

"We should get out of here." Devin's voice popped me from my panic and pulled me back to the present, to this undercover assignment.

The next thing I knew, the jostling crowds surrounded me. Everyone stampeded to exit the store as the scent of smoke filled the air. What had seemed like a smooth encounter just got bumpy. Very bumpy.

Where were Sherman and Evie? This hadn't been a part of our plan. Nope, this happening hadn't even been a blip on our radar.

Panic surged through me.

I needed to help Riley. I watched as he was pulled away. Devin led me in the opposite direction.

Devin's hand remained on my arm as we stepped out of the building. People flooded through the doors, most of them appearing irritated. A few seemed scared. Some recorded the incident on their cell cameras.

"That was interesting," Devin said once the sunlight hit our faces.

"You can say that again." I glanced around, searching for my friends. I spotted them pushing through the crowds toward me.

"Wait here, and I'll get that paperwork, okay? I might as well make the most of our time."

I nodded, and he walked away.

Well, the good news was that Devin hadn't asked me

to walk with him. But I couldn't stop thinking about Riley. Someone had set him up.

Something was going on here.

I peered through the crowds and saw Evie and Sherman coming my way. But getting through the stampede of people evacuating the grocery store was like swimming through quicksand.

As soon as the thought entered my mind, I heard a fire truck pulling in. Police cars.

Another vehicle pulled up to the curb beside me. I turned to see if it was an emergency vehicle as well.

It wasn't.

It was a van.

The back door opened, and someone grabbed me and yanked me into the back.

In the distance, I heard someone yell, "Gabby!"

Evie. That sounded like Evie.

Before I could fight, a bag covered my head, and everything went black.

A sound pulled me from the blackness.

My eyes flew open, but blackness still surrounded me.

I sucked in a breath as my heart rate surged. Everything flashed back to me.

The grocery store. The fire alarm. Feeling someone grab me.

And now this.

The rumble beneath me—the van?—stopped.

I froze as I listened.

A door opened. I could sense the light around me. Sunlight?

Rough hands grabbed my arms and jerked me out. Led me across a rocky path. Up a few stairs. My escort moved so quickly that my feet could hardly keep up.

I heard a click. A door opened—I thought. And then someone shoved me. I flew through the air and fell on a roughly carpeted floor. Something slammed.

Then silence.

I lay there. Heart pounding. Hardly able to breathe. Unsure what to expect. Still unable to see.

What had just happened?

Panic rushed through me. Memories of being abducted by a serial killer. Of being held captive. In a cabin. In a swamp.

Uncontrollable tremors captured my body. My muscles. Everything.

Whenever the memories hit, they tried to shut me down.

I couldn't afford that right now. No, right now, I had to figure out what was going on here.

"Are you okay?" someone asked.

A woman. With a soft voice. She sounded like she was right above me.

The bag covering my face moved. Tugged. And then disappeared.

I blinked a few times until . . . Brooke Murphy came into focus. She knelt beside me, looking the same yet different. No longer was she perfectly coifed. No, dark roots had come in through her blonde hair. It was wavy now and pulled back into a sloppy ponytail. Her skin looked pale, and there were bags under her eyes.

"You're . . . Brooke." I tried to push myself up, but I couldn't. My arms were bound behind me.

"You know my name?" She put her hands on my shoulders and helped me sit upright. But her lips were parted, her forehead wrinkled, and her voice contained a wisp of confusion . . . and maybe hope.

"I've been looking for you." My head pounded. Had I hit it? Or had I been drugged? I didn't know. Everything was hazy.

"For me? Why?" The confusion in her voice grew deeper, wispier.

My gaze met Brooke's. "Your husband asked me to."

Tears filled Brooke's eyes. She let out a gasp and rocked back, her hand covering her mouth. "Conrad? But they said . . ."

The truth hit me. The truth about how manipulative these guys were, and the lies they'd probably fed Brooke. They'd preyed on the fact she was compassionate, infertile, and in debt. It was deplorable.

"They probably told you Conrad moved on." My voice

cracked as I said the words. I didn't take this conversation lightly. I could only imagine what Brooke was feeling right now, especially when combined with what she'd been through.

She nodded, more moisture overflowing from her eyes and down her cheeks. "They did. They had pictures of Conrad with an old girlfriend, even."

Emily, I realized. It had to be her. "I don't believe anything happened between Conrad and Emily. I looked into it myself. They were just friends. Everyone thinks you might be dead."

A sob escaped, even though Brooke looked like she tried to hold it back. "They said if I tried to run, they'd kill Conrad and my parents. I couldn't let that happen."

"No one could blame you." These guys were the lowest of the low.

I glanced around, briefly soaking in my surroundings. It was a small, dingy space. An old hotel room? Maybe.

An orange-and-green bedspread lay across a double bed. Stained, dirty carpet stretched across the floor. A doorway gaped in the distance, no doubt a bathroom. Water stains blotched the ceiling and walls, and the whole place reeked with age and mold.

A window offered an outside view. I doubted it was breakable, however. If so, Brooke would be long gone by now.

I needed answers. But I also needed to get out of here.

"Brooke, can you get these ties off my wrists?" I pulled against my binds to no avail.

"Let me see." She crawled behind me and began working the ropes.

Finally, they released, and I rolled my shoulders, trying to gather my thoughts and get my bearings. The conclusions I drew churned my stomach. For the first time in a long time, I hoped I was wrong.

"I've been putting some of the pieces together," I started. I stood and stretched my back, I paced a three-foot area, my gaze still scanning the room as I thought out loud. Briefly, I ran my hand through my hair. It was still pinned back, but the wig was gone. "Someone approached you about taking a part-time job helping underprivileged pregnant women, correct?"

Brooke nodded, rising from the floor and moving to sit on the edge of the bed. "I went to an interview after work one day. It was out in public at the resort area. There was a festival down there that weekend, so it was busy. The next thing I knew, I was walking back to my car when a van pulled up and someone grabbed me. I ended up here. It's been . . ."

"Four months," I answered softly.

She seemed to age several years right before my eyes. "That's what I thought. You start to lose track after a while."

"I'm sure you do."

"These guys knew everything about me," Brooke

continued, more moisture filling her gaze. There were no tissues in here—that I could see—so she wiped her eyes with the back of her hand. Her voice cracked as she continued. "They'd looked into my background. Knew I was in debt. That I was desperate for money. That I liked to help people. I walked right into their trap. I didn't realize I'd made myself such an easy target."

Maybe that explained the people Conrad claimed were watching him. The man Conrad's neighbor had seen going through his mailbox. Whoever it had been, he'd been gathering information to use as leverage. Probably the same with Sir Watson. The man who'd picked him up had come into my house. What had he learned?

"I'm guessing things here aren't what they seem," I finally said. "These men are taking these babies and putting them up for adoption, aren't they?"

"They are." Brooke sounded breathless with astonishment. "It's horrible. I actually had the chance to escape once. But I couldn't leave these women. They need someone. I'm not much, but without me . . . I just don't know what would happen to them."

The severity of the situation hit me. I'd been involved in a lot of cases. But never one like this. "Who are these women?"

"Most of them don't speak English. A lot are from Eastern Europe or Central America. I overheard some of the guys talking when I first got here. Apparently, these women sign a paper after the baby is born. They think they're going to get citizenship, but they're actually signing away their rights. After the babies come, the women are shipped back to their home country, and they're basically powerless to do anything about this. It's heartbreaking. It really is."

I couldn't even begin to comprehend this. "How many women?"

"I've been here four months, you said? I've helped to deliver thirteen babies. After I do my job, the guards lock me back up in here like a prisoner. They treat the women well—until after the baby is born. Then . . . well, they're useless."

"How many pregnant women are here now?"

"Three."

I glanced around again. "There's no way out?"

"No way out. There are windows, but they're that thick, plastic stuff—polycarbonate, I think is what it's called. You can't break it."

Okay, I'd figured that. I just needed to keep thinking. "Do you know where we are?"

"It's an old hotel, best I can gather. I think we're still in Virginia Beach, maybe out in the Pungo area. There's not much development, and we're surrounded by trees."

"So people can't see this place from the street," I muttered.

"Exactly. Now, can you tell me who you are?" Brooke braced her hands on either side of her and waited.

I nodded and launched into everything that happened.

But a bad feeling remained in my gut.

This was far more serious than I'd ever guessed. All the precautions I'd put in place before meeting with Devin? I wasn't sure they'd do any good out here in the middle of nowhere.

CHAPTER TWENTY-FOUR

'd just finished telling Brooke everything when the door opened. Joseph Stephens stood there, but gone was the professional caseworker who helped make families complete. In his place was a sadistic man with money signs in his eyes—and malice. A lot of malice.

"We need to have a word with you . . . Mrs. Thomas." His voice crackled with satisfaction, almost like he was enjoying this confrontation or that he'd at least been looking forward to it.

So he knew who I really was. How long had he known? Had he meant to grab Macy today?

Even though I'd learned a lot, there was still a lot I didn't know, a lot that didn't make sense.

Before I could object, two men rushed in behind

Stephens and grabbed my arms. One of them was Scar-face. The man who'd stalked Brooke. Who'd taken Sir Watson.

I kicked and screamed, trying to stop them from manhandling me. It did no good.

The men dragged me out of the room, despite my protests.

They squeezed my arms so tightly that I could feel bruises forming. But bruises were probably the least of my concerns right now. I didn't know if I'd live through this. Because I had nothing to offer these men. I had no skills to help them in this baby "business" they had going on.

Which meant I was expendable.

My pulse hammered harder at the thought.

After walking down the musty hallway, Stephens opened another door and shoved me inside. The two men pushed me into a chair and stood on either side of me, in case I decided to try anything.

I could hardly catch my breath. My lungs were tight. My mouth went dry.

Especially when I looked down.

Blood stained the carpet around me.

I'd recognize it anywhere. I had been a crime-scene cleaner, so blood stains were my specialty. Right now, I wished they weren't. Ignorance was bliss.

My throat tightened.

"You were getting a little too close to the truth, Mrs.

Thomas." Stephens paced in front of me, a long knife in his hand.

I didn't want to think about what he was planning on using that knife for.

He was no longer dressed like a professional. No, he wore jeans and a black T-shirt that left plenty of exposed skin to show his many, many tattoos. A slight accent also crept into his voice. Was that Russian? I wasn't sure.

"I was hired to find the truth," I croaked out. "Find answers."

"We eluded the police, yet a scrappy little former crime-scene cleaner found us and came close to exposing our whole operation. If I wasn't so angry, I might be impressed."

"You researched me." I'd figured they had, but hearing it sent shivers up my spine.

"We're very thorough."

I refused to look away from the challenge in his gaze. "I'm still not sure how you knew I was going to show up today for that meeting and not Macy."

He shrugged, still examining the blade of his knife. "Maybe we didn't. Maybe it was just luck. But we've had our eye on you since you came into that pharmacy. We didn't think you'd get this far."

"You set up Riley today at the grocery store coffee shop."

"It doesn't take much to get people to do what we

want. We paid that woman fifty dollars to accuse your husband of wrongdoing. The result, for us, is priceless."

My dislike for the man grew by leaps and bounds with every passing second.

"The nurse who was found dead in the woods. Was she involved with this?"

A flicker of surprise registered in the man's gaze. "She stopped cooperating. Remember that. That's when we had to bring in Brooke."

I really disliked this guy. "There's no one you can hire to do this? You have to lure people away to work for you?"

"We find if people are our prisoners, they're much more likely to do what we want." Stephens flashed a heartless smile.

The more I heard, the more I wanted to puke. "So let me get this straight. You lure desperate women here to have their children, then you snatch babies away and put them up for adoption. The thirty-plus thousand dollars you ask for in adoption fees are basically pocketed by you and your crew. Meanwhile, these women never see their children again. You should feel like a real winner. And the fake baby at home and lack of sleep Devin mentioned at our meeting? Great detail to win people's trust."

His heartless smile turned into a satisfied one. "You got it. Though it does sound a little lacking in compassion when you say it that way. It's really a win-win for everyone. These children don't need to grow up in the kind of poverty their birth moms offer. They deserve better."

"Maybe these women should make that choice. There are worse things than being poor." The man was awfully presumptuous.

"Like what?" His question sounded honest.

"Like being ripped away from your mother, for starters."

He chuckled, his confusion disappearing faster than his morals. "You're feisty. We could use someone like you on our team."

I glanced at the men beside me, and briefly considered fighting back. I knew there was no way I could win, though. "Why am I here?"

He held the knife up to the light to better examine the razor-sharp blade. "We have to figure out what to do with you. We just knew we couldn't leave you investigating."

"I thought the police were on your side." That was what Macy had implied. That the man from the hospital had met with an officer who matched Belfield's description.

Stephens shrugged again. "You really don't need to worry about the details at this point."

I was very worried about the details at this point—the details on how to get out of here, if anyone would find me, and if my friends were okay.

"My friends aren't going to drop this, you know."

"You'd better hope they do, or we'll drop some information to implicate your friend Sherman for hacking into official US servers. He could do some serious jail time for that."

I sucked in a breath. They knew about that? "You wouldn't do that."

"Don't worry—we've already told him what the consequences will be if he continues to push this."

I swallowed hard. "You're thorough." And evil. Pure evil.

"We think of everything," Stephens said. "Don't worry—we're going to put you to good use until we figure out what to do with you. We need someone to help clean up this place, and we hear you're really good at doing that."

Was he serious? One look at his expression, and I knew he was.

"I'm not cleaning up for you."

"If you don't, there will be consequences."

"Do whatever you want. I'm not helping you." I raised my chin, a surge of anger rushing through me. I wasn't going to make their lives any easier by helping them. No way.

He stepped closer, glowering down at me and still holding his knife. "Then we'll start killing your friends. One by one. Starting with Sierra."

The fluid left my face as his words sank in. Sierra?

"And then Reef will need a mom," he continued.

Reef? He knew Reef's name?

Nausea gurgled in my gut.

He flashed a smile—a soulless smile. "Don't worry. I don't think we'll have any problems placing a cute little boy like Reef with one of our waiting families. We'll make sure we find him a good home."

CHAPTER TWENTY-FIVE

Stephens wasted no time putting me to work. And, based on the armed guard watching me— that would be Scarface—I had no choice but to comply.

For now.

Every time I thought about Reef, about Sierra, my eyes welled with tears. I would never purposefully put that boy in danger. Never.

These men knew what they were doing. They were good at manipulating. Threatening. Knowing what a person's currency was.

Despair wanted to creep in. To seize my thoughts and emotions. But I couldn't let that happen. Despair wouldn't help me figure out a solution here.

I glanced around me. The hotel room that had been cleared and turned into a temporary surgical area. A hospital bed stood in the center of it, surrounded by an IV pole and a surgical tray with various tools and plastic gloves. An old bassinet huddled in the corner.

My job was to sanitize the whole place. Using a scrub brush, I used Clorox to clean the baseboards. When I finished with that, I'd been told I'd need to scrub the walls and the bathroom and the window until there was no chance of bacteria being present in the room.

Halfway through, I stood, stretching a moment. My knees hurt. I could hardly breathe. And my hands burned from the Clorox.

My gaze hit the surgical tray in front of me. I eyeballed the scalpel there.

"Don't even think about it," Scarface muttered, watching my every move.

"I thought I might need to sanitize it," I said.

He grunted in response and then snarled. "Get back to work."

I moved across the room to start the other side. My thoughts raced as I worked.

I needed a plan.

But I was in the middle of nowhere. Without a vehicle.

And Brooke was right. How could I leave these women behind? I hadn't met any of them yet. But I'd heard them murmuring behind closed doors. I could almost feel the despair in this place.

And it bothered me down to my core. Regardless of anyone's thoughts on immigration or politics, this whole thing was just wrong on so many levels.

As I moved on to clean the windows, I paused as I glanced outside.

On the back of the property, I spotted a familiar sight.

It was a dog. Tied to a stake.

Sir Watson.

Scarface had brought Sir Watson here.

I finished cleaning the delivery room, and my entire body ached. That ache didn't begin to compare to the ache I felt in my heart, though. Ache for these women. For this situation. For my poor dog.

Scarface nudged his gun at me. "Now you can fix the ladies some food."

"I don't think they'll enjoy my cooking. Just ask my husband."

He growled. "No cooking. Sandwiches. Now get in the hallway."

I raised my hands, knowing better than to argue. He led me three doors down to yet another hotel room. This one had been set up as a supply room. Scarface nudged me toward a fridge.

"Make sandwiches."

I began pulling out supplies and putting together lunch. Or was it dinner? It had to be dinnertime.

At the thought, my stomach rumbled.

"Who usually does this?" I asked.

"What's it matter?"

"Just making conversation."

"I don't like conversation."

"I see." I fixed the rest of the food in silence and put everything in little brown bags.

This was what they planned on doing with me? Using me as a servant for however long they pleased? Until they changed their minds and killed me?

This wasn't going to work.

"Deliver the food," Scarface ordered.

I swallowed hard. This meant that I might get to interact with the women. To see them with my own eyes. A sense of both dread and excitement filled me. The dread was obvious. These women were in a horrible situation. The excitement was that I got to check out their statuses for myself. It would give me a better idea of what I needed to do here.

The first room I entered made me freeze. A very pregnant woman lay on the bed reading a magazine. These rooms were nicer, cleaner.

The moms here had no idea, did they? They thought this was normal.

My heart hurt even more.

The woman rubbed her belly and smiled at me before saying in broken English, "You bring dinner?"

I forced a smile and nodded. Scarface was in the doorway, waiting just out of sight. Did that mean they didn't show the women their guns? Their weapons? Did they fear the women would put things together and realize this was all a scam?

And where did the women go after they delivered? Didn't the pregnant moms realize something was wrong? No, these men must have a plan for that.

"Thank you for food," the woman said.

She may not be thanking me once she tasted it. Then again, it was a sandwich. I couldn't mess it up but so much.

"No problem. What's your name?"

"Juanita."

"Where are you from?"

"Cuba."

I nodded, unsure what else to say.

"You new," she said.

"I am. I'm helping around the place."

"I did that in Cuba," Juanita said. "I clean an old hotel. For . . . how you say? Vacationers. No women like me."

"Are you comfortable here?" The words burned as they left my lips.

"I am. Thank you. I thankful to be here, for better life for my child."

There was a knock at the door. Scarface. He was indicating I was taking too long.

I forced another smile. "Enjoy your food."

"I will." Juanita smiled and rubbed her stomach. "We both will."

rooke was escorted back to the room an hour or so after I returned—I didn't have a watch, so I was just guessing. She looked even more exhausted than she had earlier.

This ordeal had taken its toll on her, as it would anyone in her shoes.

Her eyes lit when she saw me. She obviously wasn't used to having a roommate, but she looked glad to no longer be alone. She went directly to the bathroom and began scrubbing her hands. Almost obsessively. Was she trying to wash away the things she'd been forced to do? How she was cooperative, but only out of concern for the women?

I stood from the bed where I'd been sitting and walked toward her. I crossed my arms and leaned against the wall, watching as she ran water over her hands, scrubbing them until they were red.

"Tough day?" I asked.

She nodded. "Yeah. Checkups to make sure the babies are doing well. Lots of questions from the moms—questions I don't know how to answer. I don't want to freak them out. Besides, the guards are always listening. They'll hear me if I tip anyone off."

Finally, Brooke turned off the water and dried her hands. Together, we walked back toward the bed. She sat on one side, and I sat on the other. Silence stretched between us a moment. There was so much to be said, yet so little that would make a difference.

I glanced at the window. It was nighttime now. The dark sky stretched on endlessly. I handed Brooke a paper bag with one of the sandwiches I made earlier. Lackluster, she opened it and pulled out her dinner.

I hadn't even been here twenty-four hours. Brooke had been here four months, locked in here day after day with little hope of escape.

My heart ached at the thought.

"I'm surprised they're keeping us together," I said.

"The other rooms are damaged," she said. "Rotting floors and such. They probably think you'd try to get away. In fact, the whole floor above us has extensive water damage. You can't walk up there without falling through the floor. That's what I overheard some of the men say, at least."

"Brooke, I have a question. How many men work here? Do you know?"

She shrugged. "Let me think. I'm pretty sure there are five of them, including Mr. Stephens and a man with a scarred face. Then there's Devin, the man who recruited me. Why?"

"Because we need to get out of here before this continues. We're expendable to them. Especially me. When they're done with us, they'll kill us."

"I can't leave these women." Her lips pulled down in a frown that consumed her entire face. "Four women left this morning, Gabby, before you arrived. I don't even know where they were taken."

Left this morning? Was that what they were talking about down at the shipping containers I'd seen? Were these women "the goods"?

The realization made nausea swell in my gut.

I couldn't dwell on that right now.

"We can bring them with us when we escape," I said.

I pulled my legs under me more tightly, feeling as if this looked too much like a slumber party when it was anything but. We weren't two girls chatting about boys and makeup. No, we were making life-or-death choices.

"One woman—Juanita—is about to deliver any time now," Brooke said, pulling a dirty pillow onto her lap. "I'm not sure we can risk traveling with her."

I remembered Juanita from when I'd delivered the food. I remembered her warm eyes that were tinged with fear. Was it the normal fear that an expecting mother felt at the thought of delivering her baby? Or was it fear because she knew something was wrong?

"Can we risk them taking away her baby?" It shouldn't even be a choice.

Brooke hung her head. "No. I . . . I just don't know what to do. I feel helpless."

Helplessness wasn't an option here. We had to stay focused on solutions. "Do you know where these guards are usually stationed?"

"There are two ways in and out of this building. There's one guard stationed in the hall and another man at the main exit. They pretty much patrol these hallways and make sure everyone stays in line."

"So there may only be two men here at certain times."

"That's correct."

"We can take out two men."

"I'm not sure how you plan on doing that. They have guns. We don't."

I wished I did have my gun. But I must have dropped my purse when they'd snatched me or these men had taken it. "It's like eating an elephant. You just have to take it one bite at a time. But there are details I need to work out first. Do you know how to unlock the doors to these women's rooms?"

"The guard in the hallway has the keys."

I'd figured that. "Perfect. So we need to take him out,

release the women from their rooms, and then we take out the guard at the exit."

Based on the knot between Brooke's eyebrows, she still wasn't convinced. "Even if that worked, how do we get away from here? These women aren't going to be able to run through the woods. At least not for very long."

"I'm sure there's a vehicle here. We take out the guards, we get the keys, we leave."

Brooke studied me, a mix of doubt and admiration in her gaze. "Are you like an ex-CIA operative or something?"

I let out a feeble laugh. "No, I'm actually a former crime-scene cleaner."

My words didn't seem to reassure her. But I was going to have to work with that.

Brooke and I had to wait for the perfect timing to plan our escape. I really wanted that to be when Stephens wasn't here. That ruled out this evening.

Besides, Brooke had been called out of the room, and I heard screams coming from down the hallway. She'd come back two hours later and told me Juanita had gone into false labor.

Then Brooke had lain in bed. I wasn't sure if she was sleeping or not. But having some time alone with my thoughts wasn't a bad thing. I'd taken a shower, but I wasn't sure if I felt cleaner or dirtier after being in the filthy bathroom. I'd hand-washed my clothes and laid them out to dry, keeping a towel around me in the meantime.

It wasn't ideal, but it had felt good to get the grime off of me from earlier. However, the smell of Clorox would remain for days to come. I was sure of it.

I paced to the window and stared outside, my thoughts going to Sir Watson. How was he? Had they fed him? Was he hurt?

The men hit the most vulnerable of our society. Pregnant women. Women from other countries, with nothing else but hope for a better life. They leveraged people's weaknesses against them. They even had no regard for animals.

When I'd started this investigation, I'd wondered what it would take for me to walk away from my life.

Now I knew.

The only thing that would make me do that was to protect the people I loved.

Riley's face flashed in my mind. Then Sierra. Then Reef.

I would do anything to ensure they were safe.

I pressed my cheeks against the cool glass a moment, my thoughts racing.

I missed Riley. I wanted to feel his arms around me. I wanted to hear his assurance that everything would be okay. I wanted to talk about the future and make plans and dream about growing old together.

He'd changed so much since we'd first met. He'd gone from being the boy next door and the man of my dreams, to suffering from the gunshot wound to the head. That had forever changed our lives, and I wasn't always sure I was ever going to get him back. But I had. And now he was finally getting his life back on track. He enjoyed his job. He was working out. He even filled in at church sometimes and preached when our pastor was out of town.

What if I never saw him again?

A cry caught in my throat.

I was ready for some kind of next step. Was that starting a family? A different career?

I still wasn't sure.

God, I'm not ready for all of this to end. I know my life here on earth is temporary. I was never meant to put my hope in it. But I just feel like I have more left.

Then again, my problems were small in comparison to the victims here.

Please, Lord, these women. Help the mothers who've lost their babies. Help the women who might be heading back to hostile countries. There's so much to pray for that I don't even know where to start. You know the situation. Please intervene.

"I wish I hadn't kept so many secrets from Conrad."

I turned and saw Brooke lying in bed, staring at the window with a lifeless look in her eyes.

"He still loves you, Brooke."

"I treasured shopping more than I treasured our marriage," she continued. "And I realized it too late. In my quest to make things right, I made things worse. So much worse."

"You couldn't have known."

"Why does it take tragedy for a person to see life clearly?"

I moved to sit on the corner of the bed. "I don't know. But that's the way it seems to work all too often."

"Do you think he'll forgive me?"

"I know he will."

Her wide eyes met mine. "Do you really think we'll get out of here?"

I carefully thought about my answer before nodding. "I do. It may not be easy. But we can do this. I promise we can."

CHAPTER TWENTY-SEVEN

At 6:00 a.m. the next morning, I watched as Joseph Stephens pulled away from the hotel. I hadn't slept all night. No, I'd bounced back and forth from pacing the floor to tossing and turning in bed. All the while, I'd been thinking, pondering, and formulating.

I knew there were other men involved with this, men like Devin. But my impression was that he handled the business side of this operation. I hadn't seen him here. Not yet.

And I hoped I didn't.

Because right now, I assumed there were only two guards here. Scarface and that other guy.

And that was still in question.

As soon as Stephens pulled away, I hopped out of bed and began to gather my supplies. Which were limited.

As Brooke pressed her ear to the door and listened for

footsteps, I managed to rip a piece of our sheets until it formed something of a rope. It would have to do.

I took a bobby pin from my hair—it was left over from my wig. Thank goodness. They came in handy at the least expected times. I pushed that into my pocket.

"How do you know all of this?" Brooke asked.

I pushed away memories that nipped at my sanity. "I was abducted by a serial killer once. I vowed never to let myself be a victim like that again. So I started studying survival skills. Developing plans. I'm not ready to die yet."

Brooke's face tightened until she finally frowned, obviously still nervous. "I can appreciate that. But what can I do?"

Good. I was making progress. "How many footsteps did you hear?"

"Just one set."

My mind raced as I thought all of this through. "And Stephens doesn't usually get back until after five?"

"That's correct . . . usually."

I nodded and stood. I didn't want to waste any more time. "We should probably get moving."

Brooke grabbed my arm before I walked away, something close to panic in her gaze. "What if this doesn't work?"

"We have to believe it will. If not, you can tell these guys that I put you up to it. Besides, they need you. Not me."

Finally, she nodded. "Let's do this, then."

On my knees, I took up residence by the doorway. I used a bobby pin to work the lock, trying to be patient. But the cockroach crawling along the wall beside me only made me want to rush.

Finally, the lock clicked. I'd done it! I'd actually practiced doing stuff like this in my spare time. Some people read books or did crossword puzzles. I worked on survival skills.

Now who was the smart one?

I'd counted the seconds between footsteps, and I knew exactly when I needed to open the door. I also knew the door didn't squeak. I also knew I didn't have much time once I set all this in place.

Brooke had one job: once the first guard was down, she needed to grab his keys and let the women out of their rooms. I would take care of the rest.

Just as I heard the footsteps pass again, I carefully turned the knob. The door didn't make a sound as I eased it open.

Perfect.

I quickly glanced down the hall. One guard came into view at the end of the hallway. His back was toward me as he paced away from our door.

I wrapped a strip of the torn bedsheet around my

hands, sneaked from the room, and crept toward the man. When I was only a foot away, I lunged toward him, latching onto his back.

"What?" he screeched.

He tried to turn but couldn't. My arms slipped in front of him, and the strip of cloth wrapped around his neck. I squeezed as hard as I could.

The man clawed at the fabric to no avail. He thrashed for a moment before ramming me into the wall. The air left my lungs, and pain rushed through my body.

But that wasn't going to slow me down.

I pulled the cloth tighter, determined that my plan would work.

He tried to slip his fingers between the fabric and skin, but it was no use. I just needed to cut off his air for ten seconds. Ten more seconds.

My muscles trembled from holding the cloth so tightly. The more the man thrashed, the harder it was to keep my grip.

The noise of our fight would no doubt alert the other guard. I didn't have much time here. If this didn't go according to plan then everything would fall apart.

Please, Lord. I could use some favor right now.

Finally, the man stopped fighting. I held my breath, waiting to see what would happen next.

He slunk to the floor. He'd passed out—for now.

I drew in a shaky breath—a breath that matched my shaky limbs.

First part of the plan, done.

I grabbed the guard's gun first and shoved it into my waistband. Then I snatched up his keys and looked back at Brooke, who'd plastered herself against the wall outside our room.

She was freezing up, I realized. I couldn't let that happen.

I tossed her the keys. "Get the ladies out."

As Brooke scrambled across the hall, I dragged the man into our room and hurried back. Once the door was closed behind me, I paused long enough to suck in several deep breaths. My heart pounded furiously in my ears. This was far from being done.

Brooke emerged down the hallway, women in tow. Each looked nervous. They whispered to each other, but I couldn't understand what they were saying.

They'd thought they'd come here for a hope of new life. Certainly, they were confused about why they were being taken from their supposedly safe environment and being forced to run.

I couldn't explain it all right now. I didn't have the time, and we had to remain quiet.

I motioned for Brooke to hand me the keys, and I locked our door—just in case the man came to. Then it was time to move.

As we approached the front door, I signaled for everyone to wait. I peered around the corner.

Scarface stood there, his weapon at his waist.

My palms felt sweaty as I held the guard's gun in my hands. I was responsible for more lives than just my own. The charge weighed heavily on my shoulders.

I could hardly breathe as I raised my weapon and aimed it at Scarface.

Quickly, I glanced back. Saw the women huddled together, clinging to each other. Saw the fear on their faces.

I had no choice but to move forward with this.

Carefully, I aimed at Scarface. I swallowed hard, praying this plan worked.

And then I pulled the trigger.

The bullet hit his knee.

Scarface howled with pain. He collapsed, blood seeping onto the floor. But his eyes still showed determination as he glowered at me.

"What do you think you're doing?"

I wanted to tell him that I had no idea. But that would get me nowhere. Instead, I crept a step closer. "This is going to be a bad day for you."

He snarled again before glancing at the weapon at his belt. "Why's that?"

"Because you're not going to be above ground." Okay, it was a bad, messed-up misuse of a movie quote from his namesake. I couldn't resist.

I rushed toward him, careful to keep my gun on him, and snatched his weapon before he could grab it.

"You don't know what you're doing," he grumbled, letting out another moan.

"I think I do," I told him. "Get up."

"You just shot my knee!"

"Get up anyway." I had no compassion for the man. He deserved everything he got. But it wasn't my job right now to be the judge and jury.

He mumbled something under his breath and limped to his feet.

"Get in there," I ordered. I pointed to an office beside him.

He gave me one last dirty look before dragging himself there. Once he was inside, I shoved a large table in front of the door. That should keep him—for a little while, at least.

"Let's go, ladies. We've got to get out of here. Now."

I opened the door and stepped outside. Just as I ushered everyone out behind me, I sensed a shadow fall over me.

"Smooth move, but you're not going anywhere."

CHAPTER TWENTY-EIGHT

I froze and turned toward the voice. I knew who it was without looking. Joseph Stephens. With a gun.

"Put your weapons down before I start shooting," he said.

I obeyed then raised my hands and turned toward him, first making sure the rest of the women were behind me. At least, I'd go down first. Maybe—hopefully—he'd spare everyone else.

The women huddled in the alcove by the front door. One of the women whimpered. Another let out a cry that turned into a sob.

I didn't have to glance behind me to know the women were huddled together, all fearing for their lives. For the lives of their unborn children.

Please, Lord . . .

"Get back inside." Joseph pointed to the door with his gun. "I should have known you'd try something like this."

"I'm not going back in there." The words surprised even me. But I hadn't come this far to march back into that old hotel.

He chuckled. "I don't think you know who you're talking to. I'm the one with the gun."

"You're going to have to kill me first." I wasn't sure what that would prove. I only knew this had to end. Drastic measures were needed here—this situation was bigger than one life—bigger than my life. If I didn't free these women, I didn't know who would.

A new gleam entered his gaze. "My pleasure."

He cocked his gun and aimed it right toward my heart.

The breath left my lungs. This was it. He was going to do it.

More sobs rose to the heavens, each more frantic than the last.

My muscles clenched as I prepared myself for the sting of the bullet. I prayed the women might run. Might escape. Might somehow find their way out of this.

Stephens stretched out his arm, and I knew I was only seconds from feeling the worst pain of my life.

Lunge at him.

No, he would just shoot me faster.

Distract him.

Chances of that helping were slim.

Bargain with him.

That might buy me some time.

Lord, what should I do?

Out of nowhere, someone appeared. Tackled Stephens to the ground.

I sucked in a breath.

That wasn't someone.

That was . . . Sir Watson.

The dog pinned Stephens down and snarled on top of him. A frayed rope hung from his collar.

Good boy. I smiled.

Sir Watson's assistance had definitely bought me some time.

I didn't have time to praise the canine now. No, I grabbed the gun that had flown out of Stephens's hand, and I aimed it at the ringleader of this whole dirty operation.

"Stay right there, Sir Watson," I murmured. "Don't go anywhere."

"Get this dog off me!" Stephens yelled, pressing himself into the ground with enough force that he added a couple of chins at his neckline.

"Stay, Watson." I glanced at Stephens. "And his teeth are really sharp, just in case you're wondering."

"I think my water just broke!" one of the women behind me yelled.

Labor? Juanita was going into labor in the middle of all this?

My stress level crept higher and higher.

"Brooke, can you help her?" I called over my shoulder.

"Of course." Brooke rushed toward the woman.

There was no way we'd be escaping on foot, not with a baby coming. This seriously limited my options.

I glanced to my left and saw a truck. Stephens must have driven it. But it would hold only three at the most. The back was loaded with wood and other junk, making it look like a construction vehicle almost.

The tension in my shoulders stretched with more force as Juanita screamed in pain again. I needed to think of a plan and quickly.

I couldn't leave the rest of the women here. It was too risky.

With my gun still trained on Stephens and Sir Watson still snarling on top of him, I reached toward the man and grabbed the cell phone from his pocket. I called the police, and they promised they were on their way.

I stared at the phone a moment, tempted to call Riley. But I didn't have time for that now. I needed to make sure these women were safe. The men inside could easily come to or call in reinforcements. I hadn't intended to linger any longer than necessary.

Juanita screamed behind us. I glanced back long enough to see her holding her stomach. To see the sweat pouring down her face, and the panic in her gaze.

"The baby is coming!" she yelled. "Now!"

I had to figure out a plan, and I had no time to waste.

CHAPTER TWENTY-NINE

*J*ust then, a car pulled up and the passenger door flung open. "Get in!"

I peered inside at the person in the driver's seat. "Macy?"

"Come on! We don't have much time." Macy motioned wildly, indicating we should climb in.

"How'd you find us?" I asked, my throat tightening.

"It's a long story. I don't have time to explain now. Come on."

I could sense the women behind me running toward the vehicle, and I raised my arms to block them. "We're not going with you, Macy."

Her smile dimmed. "Why wouldn't you? I'm here to help. I've risked everything."

"You can help by stepping out of the car and handing me the keys."

"Don't you want to get away from here?" Macy stared at me like I'd lost my mind.

"Macy?" Brooke ran toward the car. "Is that you?"

"Don't get in, Brooke," I warned.

Brooke froze and turned to look at me. "Why not?"

"Because Macy is in on this." I raised my gun. "She's the one who told these men about you. Who picked out the targets. And she's trying to capture you again."

Brooke's wide eyes went to her friend. "Macy?"

Macy didn't say anything. Instead, she jammed her foot on the accelerator, trying to take off. To get away.

But before she could, several police cars pulled up and blocked the lane leading to the hotel.

Macy's door flew open. She sprang out and began to sprint away. But Detective Belfield emerged from his car and stopped her in three strides.

Help was here. Help was really here.

And I had no confidence in Macy's accusation that the detective was in on this. No, the woman had fed me one lie after another. I'd only realized it too late.

For the past two hours, I'd given my statement to the police and the FBI. Then given my statement to them again.

An ambulance had come—actually three. Each of the

women were being helped and attended to medically. Thank goodness.

Juanita was definitely in labor. She refused to go to the hospital—probably because she was in the country illegally—so Brooke stayed with her. I could hear her screams in the distance as I stood in the lobby of the old hotel.

The good news was that the police had captured all the men here.

Sir Watson nuzzled my hand, as if reminding me he was here and he was okay. He'd faithfully stayed at my side since the police had taken over. One of the officers had even gotten the dog some water and food.

I glanced out the window, taking another sip from my water bottle. My pulse quickened when I spotted a car coming down the lane.

A familiar car.

Riley's car.

I ran outside, past the officers there, and toward the vehicle. It came to a stop in a cloud of dust, and the doors opened.

My friends came into sight.

My excitement made all my limbs feel like gelatin. They were here. They were okay.

Watson barked in excitement beside me as Riley, Sherman, and Evie all stepped out. All three threw their arms around me—even Evie.

"We were so worried," Riley said, not letting go of my waist.

"I was worried also." Holding Riley had never felt so good. "What happened?"

"You first," Evie stepped back, her eyes warmer than I'd ever seen them.

She'd really been worried about me, I realized. I didn't point it out, but satisfaction warmed me.

I told them everything, Riley holding onto me the whole time, as if afraid I might fall down or disappear. When I was done, I shrugged—not because I didn't care but because all of this felt like a nightmare.

"And that's what happened," I said.

"Wait—so Macy was a part of this?" Evie asked.

My stomach clenched as I remembered the scene. "Her job was to recruit people and to gain their trust. She scoped out people at the hospital, and she tried to control the narrative by reaching out to me. I can't believe I fell for it."

Riley squeezed my arm. "She was good at what she did. Besides, the police have her now. She won't be preying on innocent people any longer."

I knew his words were true, but it would take a while to come to terms with that deception. "All right, you heard what happened to me. Now it's your turn. What did I miss?"

"We finally convinced the police to let me go and that I had nothing to do with the smoke bomb at the grocery store," Riley said. "They had to watch the security camera footage before they would believe me."

"Did they catch the woman who accused you?" I asked.

"They did, and she admitted to being paid off," Riley said. "Then I called Parker."

Parker was my former boyfriend, and he was FBI. I'd seen him show up here. He'd nodded at me, muttered a few words, and then continued to work this scene. Seeing him wasn't surprising—this was the area he worked.

"He got the ball rolling on the investigation," Riley said. "But everything was moving entirely too slow."

"We were up all night," Evie said. "We did everything we could to find you. We checked the cell phone footage people took at the grocery store, we tried to trace the license plate number. We even went to the adoption agency and tried to get information from them. They were tightlipped."

"Parker was in the process of following the traffic cams and trying to track you down that way," Riley added. "They lost you as soon as the van you were in went outside of the metro area limits."

"Are we in Pungo?" I asked, wanting to verify that assumption.

Riley nodded. "Yeah, almost down in North Carolina. I guess this is an old hotel that never got off the ground. It closed fifteen years ago. Locals thought a construction company had bought it in hopes of fixing it up. These guys even used some of those magnetic signs on their vehicles to make people think that's exactly what they were doing. Pretty smart, actually. Otherwise, people would get suspicious over all the activity here."

Yes, they were a little too smart for their own good.

"Has anyone caught Devin?" I asked.

"I think the police have a lead on him. I have no doubt he'll be caught soon."

Shouting sounded behind me. I jogged over to one of the officers nearby. He was on his radio. What had happened?

"Juanita had her baby," the officer said. "A healthy baby boy. One who won't be taken from his mother."

Relief flushed through me. Juanita was okay. Her baby was okay. And this nightmare just might be over.

Thank You, Jesus.

"What's going to happen to all those other babies?" I asked, my heart wrenching at the thought of everyone who'd been hurt—and everyone who would still be hurt by this scheme Stephens and the gang had going.

"I don't know," Riley said, glancing behind me at the scene. "The authorities are going to have to work that out."

"They didn't kill the mothers after they delivered, did they?" Sherman asked, blinking rapidly as if he couldn't handle the thought.

I couldn't handle it either.

"I don't think so," I said. "Some of these women—

most of them—were from other countries. These men convinced them to come here to have their babies because then their child would be an American citizen. Like a birthing hotel, almost."

"I've heard of those in California," Evie said. "But I've never seen one with my own eyes."

"Politics aside, the difference between a birthing hotel and this place is that once the baby came, these men had the mothers sign a paper. They told the moms they were signing for citizenship rights. Instead, they were signing away the rights to their child."

"That's horrible," Sherman said.

"It is," I agreed. "After the mother had a few days to recover, I believe they put her in a shipping container and sent her back to her home country. She wouldn't dare speak out for fear of being in trouble for what she did. I think the men picked countries that have regimes at the helm—regimes that wouldn't smile upon what was being done."

"It sounds all around horrific," Riley said.

"I agree." I glanced back at the hotel and shuddered. "The good news is that now this is over. Maybe justice can finally be done."

Parker strode from the hotel and joined us. He extended his hand toward me, his face dead serious.

Hesitantly, I returned the gesture, but I had no idea what was going on. "What's that for?"

"Good job, Gabby." Parker's voice matched his face. "I

know I tell you not to interfere with police work. But your nosiness did good things today. Men like the ones working this operation . . . They deserve to go away for a long time. And they will. Macy also."

"I'm glad I could help."

Our attention traveled to a new vehicle that pulled up.

Conrad, I realized.

He threw the car into park. He glanced around, scanning everyone around him.

A police officer approached, trying to stop him, but Conrad ignored him. Instead, he ran toward the hotel.

I held my breath, watching what would play out.

Brooke ran from the front door of the hotel, rushing toward him.

The two embraced.

Maybe things would work out, after all, between those two. Maybe this case would get its happy ending. That was my prayer.

CHAPTER THIRTY

*T*he next morning, I stood in my front yard, with Sir Watson by my side, and waited for Evie and Sherman to arrive.

Sir Watson was becoming a permanent part of my life. Riley and I had officially adopted the pooch and set up a space for him in the corner of the living room.

The dog had saved my life, and no one had claimed him. So it seemed he was a godsend and a guardian.

I patted the top of his head. And I wasn't complaining. He'd won a place in my heart, despite my own wishes.

Evie and Sherman pulled up in their rental car and wandered toward me. I spotted their suitcases in the back-seat of the sedan, and a wash of melancholy filled me. It was time for them to leave. Again. A small part of me would miss them.

"Thank you both for coming," I started. "I'll mail your

checks."

"The money isn't really important," Evie said. "Just knowing we stopped an operation like that one is all the satisfaction I need."

"I agree," Sherman said. "Sometimes you can't put a price on justice. It's just enough in itself."

"Oh, and good news. I heard this morning that the police found Devin. He's been arrested, and the whole operation is officially shut down. The police have enough evidence to put these guys away for a long time. I couldn't have done this without you."

"Oh, I think you could have," Evie said. "But maybe we helped speed the process along. At least, we can say it was a clean sweep. The authorities caught all those guys, and they'll get what's coming to them. We also saved a lot of heartache for these women."

"I agree. It was a clean sweep."

"When's our next cold case?" Sherman asked.

"I don't know," I said. "I'll be on the lookout for it, though. For sure. And, in the meantime, I need to unpack my house, get some new furniture, and paint."

"I'd rather work on a cold case myself," Evie said.

"Me too." We shared a smile.

"What about Brooke? Any update on her involvement?" Sherman asked.

"Apparently Macy hacked into Brooke's work computer, and Macy was the one who created those fake patient files. The doctor confirmed it."

"Macy really was a wolf in sheep's clothing." Evie shook her head but looked halfway impressed at the woman's skill.

Macy *had* been impressive, but maybe her cockiness had ultimately led to her downfall. After all, she'd even given me that clue about Scarface, probably thinking I would never actually find him. Or maybe she was toying with me the whole time. I didn't know—and I probably wouldn't know since I never planned on speaking with her again.

And the woman had known I'd talked to Detective Belfield and she'd planted doubt in my mind about him, as well. Clever move on her part.

"Anyway, Brooke has been cleared of any wrongdoing," I said.

"More good news," Sherman said.

Evie glanced at her watch. "Well, we've got flights to catch. But thanks again for asking us to help."

"Thank you both again. I'll see you soon."

"We'll look forward to it," Sherman said.

We hugged again, and they departed.

This cold-case squad wasn't as bad as I thought. I mean, sure, we had our moments. But overall, we made a good team. Kind of like the crew from *Law and Order*. If they were to go on Jerry Springer.

Or like argan oil and my curly hair—it was the new peanut butter and jelly.

ALSO BY CHRISTY BARRITT:

the hidden currents surrounding her pull her under for good?

Flood Watch

The tide is high, and so is the danger on Lantern Beach. Still in hiding after infiltrating a dangerous gang, Cassidy Livingston just has to make it a few more months before she can testify at trial and resume her old life. But trouble keeps finding her, and Cassidy is pulled into a local investigation after a man mysteriously disappears from the island she now calls home. A recurring nightmare from her time undercover only muddies things, as does a visit from the parents of her handsome ex-Navy SEAL neighbor. When a friend's life is threatened, Cassidy must make choices that put her on the verge of blowing her cover. With a flood watch on her emotions and her life in a tangle, will Cassidy find the truth? Or will her past finally drown her?

Storm Surge

A storm is brewing hundreds of miles away, but its effects are devastating even from afar. Laid-back, loose, and light: that's Cassidy Livingston's new motto. But when a makeshift boat with a bloody cloth inside washes ashore near her oceanfront home, her detective instincts shift into gear . . . again. Seeking clues isn't the only thing on her mind—romance is heating up with next-door neighbor and former Navy SEAL Ty Chambers as well. Her heart wants the love and stability she's longed for her entire life. But her hidden identity only leads to a tidal wave of turbulence. As more answers emerge about the boat, the danger around her rises, creating a treacherous swell that threatens to reveal her past. Can Cassidy mind her own business, or will the storm surge of violence and corruption that has washed ashore on Lantern Beach leave her life in wreckage?

Dangerous Waters

Danger lurks on the horizon, leaving only two choices: find shelter or flee. Cassidy Livingston's new identity has begun to feel as comfortable as her favorite sweater. She's been tucked away on Lantern Beach for weeks, waiting to testify against a deadly gang, and is settling in to a new life she wants to last forever. When she thinks she spots someone malevolent from her past, panic swells inside her. If an enemy has found her, Cassidy won't be the only one who's a target. Everyone she's come to love will also be at risk. Dangerous waters threaten to pull her into an overpowering chasm she may never escape. Can Cassidy survive what lies ahead? Or has the tide fatally turned against her?

Perilous Riptide

Just when the current seems safer, an unseen danger

emerges and threatens to destroy everything. When Cassidy Livingston finds a journal hidden deep in the recesses of her ice cream truck, her curiosity kicks into high gear. Islanders suspect that Elsa, the journal's owner, didn't die accidentally. Her final entry indicates their suspicions might be correct and that what Elsa observed on her final night may have led to her demise. Against the advice of Ty Chambers, her former Navy SEAL boyfriend, Cassidy taps into her detective skills and hunts for answers. But her search only leads to a skeletal body and trouble for both of them. As helplessness threatens to drown her, Cassidy is desperate to turn back time. Can Cassidy find what she needs to navigate the perilous situation? Or will the riptide surrounding her threaten everyone and everything Cassidy loves?

Deadly Undertow

The current's fatal pull is powerful, but so is one detective's will to live. When someone from Cassidy Livingston's past shows up on Lantern Beach and warns her of impending peril, opposing currents collide, threatening to drag her under. Running would be easy. But leaving would break her heart. Cassidy must decipher between the truth and lies, between reality and deception. Even more importantly, she must decide whom to trust and whom to fear. Her life depends on it. As danger rises and answers surface, everything Cassidy thought she knew is tested. In order to survive, Cassidy must take drastic measures and end the battle against the ruthless gang DH-7 once and for all. But if her final mission fails, the consequences will be as deadly as the raging undertow.

HOLLY ANNA PALADIN MYSTERIES:

When Holly Anna Paladin is given a year to live, she embraces her final days doing what she loves most—random acts of kindness. But when one of her extreme good deeds goes horribly wrong, implicating Holly in a string of murders, Holly is suddenly in a different kind of fight for her life. She knows one thing for sure: she only has a short amount of time to make a difference. And if helping the people she cares about puts her in danger, it's a risk worth taking.

THE WORST DETECTIVE EVER:

I'm not really a private detective. I just play one on TV.

Joey Darling, better known to the world as Raven Remington, detective extraordinaire, is trying to separate herself from her invincible alter ego. She played the spunky character for five years on the hit TV show *Relentless*, which catapulted her to fame and into the role of Hollywood's sweetheart. When her marriage falls apart, her finances dwindle to nothing, and her father disappears, Joey finds herself on the Outer Banks of North Carolina, trying to piece together her life away from the limelight. But as people continually mistake her for the character she played on TV, she's tasked with solving real life crimes . . . even though she's terrible at it.

#1 Ready to Fumble

ABOUT THE AUTHOR

USA Today has called Christy Barritt's books "scary, funny, passionate, and quirky."

Christy writes both mystery and romantic suspense novels that are clean with underlying messages of faith. Her books have won the Daphne du Maurier Award for Excellence in Suspense and Mystery, have been twice nominated for the Romantic Times Reviewers' Choice Award, and have finaled for both a Carol Award and Foreword Magazine's Book of the Year.

She is married to her Prince Charming, a man who thinks she's hilarious—but only when she's not trying to be. Christy is a self-proclaimed klutz, an avid music lover who's known for spontaneously bursting into song, and a road trip aficionado.

When she's not working or spending time with her family, she enjoys singing, playing the guitar, and exploring small, unsuspecting towns where people have no idea how accident-prone she is.

Find Christy online at:

www.christybarritt.com

www.facebook.com/christybarritt

www.twitter.com/cbarritt

Sign up for Christy's newsletter to get information on all of her latest releases here: **www.christybarritt.com/ newsletter-sign-up/**

If you enjoyed this book, please consider leaving a review.